Gluttony Bay

ALSO BY MATT WALLACE

GLUTTONY
BAY

MATT WALLACE

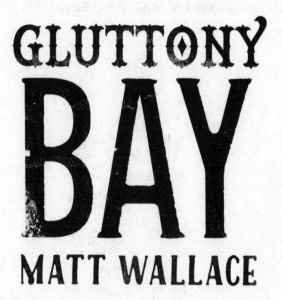

A TOM DOHERTY ASSOCIATES BOOK

NEW YORK

This is a work of fiction. All of the characters, organizations, and events portrayed in this novella are either products of the author's imagination or are used fictitiously.

GLUTTONY BAY

Copyright © 2017 by Matt Wallace

Cover illustration by Peter Lutjen
Cover design by Christine Foltzer

Edited by Lee Harris

A Tor.com Book
Published by Tom Doherty Associates
175 Fifth Avenue
New York, NY 10010

www.tor.com

Tor® is a registered trademark of
Macmillan Publishing Group, LLC.

ISBN 978-0-7653-9321-0 (ebook)
ISBN 978-0-7653-9322-7 (trade paperback)

First Edition: November 2017

Resist

PART I

FALLING OUT

WELCOME HOME

The courtyard outside may be covered in snow, but Jett Hollinshead has transformed Sin du Jour's lobby into a tropical paradise. Living palm trees potted in decorative stands mask most of the white walls, and a wave machine fills the space with the seagull-song and wind-and-wave chorus of the ocean. A rear projector has transformed the ceiling veneer into deep blue sky welcoming a brilliant morning sun through perfectly formed clouds. The rest of the space has been filled with wicker lounge furniture upholstered in nautical colors.

The chefs of Sin du Jour, including Bronko, have all donned Hawaiian floral resort shirts for the occasion. The members of Stocking & Receiving abstained, although Ryland, their resident alchemist, already half-unconscious in a cabana lounge chair, agreed to sloppily adorn a pineapple-encumbered Tommy Bahama creation. The chefs have also taken machetes to several dozen coconuts in aid of the colorful drinks being passed around in their shells.

Jett has finished off the theme by arming Moon's new

roommate: a monstrous incarnation of Cupid recently defected from Hell, who has now traded in its harp for a ukulele.

The cherubic demon expat is surprisingly adept at playing soothing island chords.

Almost the entire Sin du Jour family has gathered to welcome back Pacific and Mr. Mirabel, their intrepid veteran servers and busboys, both of whom were released from government custody the night before. They were scheduled to arrive in New York the following morning, and should be crossing into Long Island City any moment.

Jett was released a week ago from a women's holding facility in West Virginia. All she's said of her post-inauguration experience is that her cell desperately needed a coat of mint-green paint.

Of Darren there's been not a single report. Not even Bronko knows where he is or what's been done to him since the night he attempted to assassinate Enzo Consoné, now President of the Sceadu.

Darren isn't the only one from whom there's been no word, even if he's the one who the crew is most concerned about. Ritter has been on sabbatical since that same night, and though his sudden exit seems to have Bronko's unspoken approval, not even his own team has heard from him in weeks. The subject is never raised in mixed company, however—especially around Lena. The very mention of Ritter's name is still enough to send her steaming from the room on juggernaut autopilot.

White Horse and Little Dove have also been out of touch for longer than Bronko cares to think about. As far as he knows, they're still somewhere in the Southwest, on whatever personal family business took them away in the first place. He was never clear on the reason but knew enough not to pry.

Bronko has spent all morning frying and mashing up plantains along with fresh garlic, sea salt, and oil in an authentic pilón he brought back from a trip to Puerto Rico. He tasked Lena with turning the finest pork belly into perfectly fried chicharrón, while James, though still operating with only one functioning arm, crews a pot of rich, house-made chicken broth. Both ingredients will finish the perfectly formed spheres Bronko has fashioned from his plantain mixture. Together, they've all made enough mofongo (Mr. Mirabel's favorite native dish) to cater a legal cockfight on Saturday night in San Juan.

Dorsky and the rest of the line are responsible for preparing Pacific's favorite dishes. Tenryu, the kitchen's often underutilized (particularly if you believe his constant inaudible grumbling) master sushi chef, has filled taco shells with luscious hamachi, diced jalapeño, and micro-cilantro, and topped each with three equal, symmetrical dollops of crème fraîche.

Dorsky, in his very important role as sous chef and Bronko's right hand, and Rollo, in his equally important capacity as Dorsky's loyal toady, drove to the corner store to purchase Funyuns and Oatmeal Cream Pies in bulk.

To Dorsky's credit, he hasn't once complained.

In the main kitchen, Lena is cleaning her knives and watching Bronko plate his thirtieth ball of mashed, fried plantains. He places the plate on a prep station lined with the others, where they'll await finishing with the chicken broth.

"What's on your mind, Tarr?" he asks without a break in his plating or concentration. "Or what isn't on your mind, as I imagine it's a shorter list?"

Lena glances over his shoulder at James, alternately tending to his broth and cleaning up his station, as much the worker with one arm as most of the line is with two.

"Is this really the time for a party, Chef?" she asks Bronko quietly.

"It may well be the last reason we have to celebrate something for a long time," he calmly replies. "In my experience, you take such opportunities as they lay."

"Not all of us are in a celebrating mood, Chef."

"All the more reason, then."

"Chef—"

Bronko looks up from his current plating, the hard

stare of his dark, weathered eyes silencing her.

"Tarr, we got no reason to assume Vargas is any worse off than Jett or Pacific and Mo, and they're all fine. We'll get him back. I promise you. In the meantime, drivin' yerself and me crazy is what I'd call counterproductive. Savvy?"

Lena takes a deep breath, holds it, and attempts to expel every alternative reply when she exhales.

"Yes, Chef."

The clacking of stiletto heels announces Jett's presence before she rounds the archway into the kitchen, shouting, "They're here! They're here! The taxi just pulled up! Quick, everyone to the lobby!"

Jett punctuates her statement by clapping her hands twice, thunderously, and even Lena jumps at the sound.

"Yes, ma'am!" Bronko calls out obediently, throwing a wink at Tarr.

Lena wants to smile, but she just can't.

Instead, she calls out to James. "The broth will keep, James. Let's go."

He nods, in the same silent malaise that's possessed him since he awoke after being stabbed through the shoulder by the love of his life.

Lena frowns. She's tried talking to him several times, and all it has elicited are a brief, haunted smile and an empty reassurance he's all right.

In the lobby, everyone save Ryland, who no longer has the ability, stands at the ready. Bronko, Lena, and James join them. Hara, towering two heads above even Bronko and Dorsky, holds aloft a gleaming welcome home banner Jett had professionally printed. Moon sits beside Cupid, his iPhone playing island accompaniment to the former demon assassin's ukulele chords.

As they join the crowd, Lena locks eyes with Cindy for a brief moment. Lena again tries to smile, but even if she could make it happen, Cindy's stiff single nod in reply would eradicate the expression. Things have been tense between them since Lena confronted Ritter and quite literally beat him up over his role in Darren's corruption by Allensworth. Cindy's loyalty to Ritter is an absolute, and even if she does acknowledge his fault, it does nothing to warm her toward Lena for driving him away from Sin du Jour and his team.

Pacific enters the lobby like a gentle breeze, as is his way. He's swimming in an oversized parka, his mop of blond hair tied back into a ponytail, which is unusual for him. He's even acquired an uncustomary amount of barely visible beard scruff on his cheeks and jaw. It must be a side effect of weeks of prison grooming.

Pacific has not, however, lost a millimeter of that perpetual easy smile.

"'Sup, brahs?" he says.

Any individual words are swallowed in the cacophony of greetings that follows. Bronko is the first to swallow Pacific in a bear hug, while the rest crowd around the duo to welcome the kid back affectionately.

"You look good, boy," Bronko says after he's released Pacific and the voices around them have died down.

Lena is the first one to really absorb the fact Pacific appears to have arrived all alone.

"Where's Mr. Mirabel?" she asks Pacific.

It's such a stark deviation from his usual self that the briefest of flickers in Pacific's smile might as well be agonized sobbing.

"Mo. Yeah. Mo, he . . . he's gone on to that big-ass eternal rave in the sky."

They all fall silent, with their faces flat and wiped clean of their previous joy.

"Wait, what?" Lena presses.

"He died," Pacific says, reaching into the pockets of his parka and removing a joint and a Bic lighter. "A few nights ago, in the cell we were sharing. I was with him. No worries, brah."

Pacific sparks the joint and takes a few probing tokes.

"Oh, no," Nikki says, clutching her chest. "Not Mr. Mirabel."

"What did they do?" Lena demands, her words far more accusation than question.

Pacific shakes his head emphatically. "It wasn't like that, soldier. I swear. They didn't do anything to us. They fed us on the reg, brought us water whenever we asked. I even smoked out with a couple of the night guards. They were crunchy dudes, mostly."

"Then what happened, Pac?" Bronko asks, far more gently.

Pacific draws a long bomb off his joint and exhales gratefully towards the sky-camouflaged ceiling. It's the first and only time Bronko hasn't stopped him from toking in the office on sight.

"He woke up one night hacking worse than usual," Pacific recalls. "Just coughin' and coughin'. He couldn't get any air. We cranked his oxy tank all the way up. Didn't help. I guess ol' Mo's lungs just swelled shut on him, finally. He always said it would happen."

No one seems to know what to say to that, not even Bronko.

Somewhere in the back of the crowd, Dorsky disappears down the main hall off the lobby.

Pacific reaches inside his parka, digging around for several moments as if the interior were an entire junk closet. His hand finally emerges, holding several sheets of rolling papers upon which words and numbers have been scrawled in pencil by an obviously shaky hand.

Pacific offers them to Bronko.

"Mo wanted his back pay to go to his kids, along with his savings. He wrote down all the pertinents and what-not and asked me to give them to you, boss. He knew you'd handle that business."

Bronko accepts the makeshift will and testament gladly, nodding. "O' course I will. Whatever he wanted."

"Mr. Mirabel had children?" Nikki asks.

Pacific shrugs. "I guess. He never said much about 'em, or about the past, really. I don't guess they talked much. I don't guess Mo was much of a dad back in the day. I think he felt bad about that, 's why he never talked about it."

"He was a good dad to you," Nikki insists.

Pacific tries to laugh, but it comes out all wrong and he quickly abandons the gesture.

"Nah," he says. "Mo was my buddy. He was—"

The next word is lost under a wave of convulsions as Pacific, the untouchable Zen soul they've witnessed walk through carnage and chaos unscathed time and again, breaks down before them all. The tears roll over his cheeks, impossibly thick streams running down his small face as his head half-disappears into the collar of his parka.

Nikki, the breaking of her heart drawn on her face, rushes forward and practically engulfs Pacific in her embrace. He clings to her and cries into her neck for several moments.

Somewhere in the background, a lone ukulele continues to strum along. Several distressed heads turn in its direction, and Moon quickly slaps at Cupid's hands to still their playing.

"Sorry," he says to the party at large, adding quickly, "This is a bummer."

"He was a cool old man," Cindy agrees.

Pacific, more composed, tilts his face up from the crook of her neck to regard Bronko.

"Mo told me to tell you thanks, boss," he says. "He said workin' here was the best time of his whole life."

"How could he say that?" Lena asks in genuine disbelief, near tears herself. "After everything that's happened to us—"

"He was just a li'l old Puerto Rican man from Bed-Stuy," Pacific reminds her in his unruffled way. "He didn't have any friends or family. He worked in a cigar store till he couldn't breathe the air no more. He would've died alone in a rat-hole apartment without us, years ago prolly. But here? Here, he got to . . . brah, he blew up the Presidential meat puppet in front of a million people!"

"There weren't a million people at that inauguration," Cindy chimes in. "Not even close."

"Still!" Pacific insists. "Mo got to be in a battle between demon clans from hell. He got to go to Hollywood and party with celebs and he was almost burned alive except three tons of vanilla frosting fell from the ceiling. A fucked-up merman puked all over him in front of dragons made of fire and a bunch of Japanese dudes made of gnomes. He met an angel. He got to meet an actual, real angel. He got to know there was more out there than anyone else ever knows."

Pacific looks directly into Lena's eyes, and she feels herself humbled in a way she can't recall.

"Lena, brah, all the bad stuff that happens here happens out there in the normal world all the time. And worse. Way worse. Mo saw all of that too. He saw enough to know we're lucky because we get to see the other side, the magic and the shiny stuff, and it's *real*."

"Wonders," Nikki offers in a quiet voice.

Pacific nods even more emphatically. "Maybe they didn't make Mo's life worth it, but they made his goin' out worth it, and he needed that. More than anything, I think. And he was grateful for it."

Dorsky returns to the lobby with a bottle of whiskey and a tray filled with enough shot glasses for everyone in the lobby. He sets it down on the reception desk and begins pouring a finger into each glass.

No one says anything, not even Lena. They all silently and instinctively rise and gather around reception. Cindy drags Ryland to his feet and forces him along with her. Lena looks up at Bronko uncertainly, and he nods, motioning her to join the others.

Dorsky hands out shot glasses until everyone is holding his or her own, him included.

Bronko is the first to raise his glass.

"Mauricio Mirabel," he begins. "Mo to his friends. He was kitchen staff. In my day, we were taught that means family, however fucked-up and dysfunctional that family may be."

Most of the line laughs, even if it's fleeting.

"I ain't gonna pretend I knew Mo like you did, Pac," Bronko continues, "but I know one thing about the man for sure. He had no fear left. I saw that every gig we worked. Mo lived with death every day. It was part of him. And he knew it. And knowing that meant he was free to live life. I mean really live it. In the end, to my mind, that's the only real freedom there is. And I see a grace in that. There was grace in Mo."

Bronko looks to Pacific, nodding slightly.

Pacific raises his shot glass. "To Mo! Party eternal, brah!"

The rest of them toast Mr. Mirabel heartily, knocking back their fiery drinks.

In the aftermath, letting the whiskey sting their throats, everyone seems to turn inward, reflecting on mortality through their own lens.

Bronko is the first to break the silence. "Well, now, I

guess what we have on our hands here is a wake. Anybody else for eatin' and drinkin' their feelings?"

There are no dissenters, and the smell of mofongo wafting from the main kitchen is still undeniably intoxicating.

"Tarr, you up for service?" Bronko asks Lena.

She nods, slamming her glass down on the reception desk.

"Take the opportunities as they lay, right?"

"You bet, Chef," Bronko assures her.

And despite the black news, despite the specter of death hanging over the affair, it will be one of the last truly good times for the Sin du Jour crew as the makeshift family they are, feasting and laughing and crying and talking together.

It will also be the last time they all see each other alive.

FAR FROM HOME

Anywhere else in the country, a man with the lower body of a goat performing the Brazilian martial art of capoeira would undoubtedly draw the wrong kind of attention to the hidden world of the supernatural.

That's why such fights are held in New Jersey. Everything is legal in New Jersey.

A boxing ring has been erected on the dance floor of the Schuetzen Park Ballroom in North Bergen. It's a dimly lit, private affair (although the only invitation required is that you know the event is happening). The crowd is an even mix of humans and nonhumans. Being not far from the dry green expanse of the Pine Barrens, a lot of the audience is wee folk, mostly Scottish and Irish imports from the days of buckle hats and leaky sailboats.

Dozens of Alven water fairies encased in bubbles float above the crowd, enjoying a bird's-eye view of the action. There's a group of Chinese businessmen who are actually composed of several hundred Gnomi interlinked together and wearing pieces of each visitor's veneer. They all come to bet on the fights, some with hard currency, some betting magic in exchange for hard currency, or vice versa.

The Sceadu frown on such events but generally ignore them as long as the right people (or non-people) receive the appropriate consideration.

It's past eleven p.m. when the referee steps to the middle of the ring to begin the next battle. He's a goblin who was a big television star in the 1970s, until he ran afoul of the Goblin King. His punishment was the most severe in the goblin world; he was cursed to age like a normal human. Forty years later, you can scarcely see the devastatingly beautiful creature that once existed beneath several layers of wrinkles and fat and grey.

The referee calls the next two combatants to the center of the ring. Ritter is stripped to the waist, his feet bare and his hands and fists wrapped in athletic tape. It's his third fight of the night, and his dark hair is pasted to his scalp with sweat. There's a small cut across the bridge of his nose, but he's otherwise unscathed.

His opponent is a satyr with a bronze, rippling torso and long dark curls. They match the color of his woolly legs, both of which end in polished, amber hooves.

"You both know the rules," the referee reminds them. "There ain't none. You fight till one of you can't get up or gives up. We clear?"

Both opponents nod silently.

"All right, get to it!" the aged goblin instructs them.

Ritter immediately begins moving his feet in time with the satyr's ginga, the constant, repetitive dancelike movements that are the basis of capoeira. From the ginga a skilled mestre can launch spinning kicks with utterly devastating momentum behind them. Not to mention hooves are a great deal harder than human feet.

Ritter tosses out a few quick, retracting jabs experimentally. Timing an opponent who is in constant motion like this one can be extremely difficult. He decides to wait and counterstrike.

Sweeping one of his hind legs far back, the satyr springs forward and launches the first of three lightning-fast spin kicks. Ritter ducks the first, then the second, popping up and quickly meeting the third with a windmill kick of his own. Their legs meet in midair. The satyr's goatlike limb is more powerful, and the impact hurts Ritter like hell, but it succeeds in stopping his opponent's momentum and momentarily throws the half-man off-balance.

Ritter rushes forward while the satyr's back is exposed to him, but he's made the very human mistake of forgetting what he's fighting. The satyr recovers before Ritter can close the distance, and rather than waste time turning around, the creature leans forward and places both hands against the canvas mat, mule-kicking Ritter square in the chest with both hooves.

Pain sizzles both atop and beneath Ritter's skin, and the impact sends him careening backward into the ropes of the ring. He bounces off of them and charges forward at his opponent, who has already returned to the familiar motions of his *ginga*. Ritter feints quickly to the satyr's right and then leaps into the air, both feet leaving the canvas as he delivers a spinning aerial kick to the left side of the satyr's head.

Both Ritter's feet and his opponent's body touch down on the canvas at the same time. The referee quickly leans over the satyr's inert form, checking for signs of consciousness. With no signs of movement, the goblin waves his arms, signaling an end to the bout and declaring Ritter the winner.

The reaction of the crowd is mixed and largely based upon whether or not the patron had their money on Ritter. But there are many cheers; it's his third dominant performance of the night, and this crowd knows talent when they see it.

Ritter climbs down from the ring, his breathing shallow and the receding adrenaline rush leaving his blood cool. A group of perhaps a dozen small, round, mud-covered boggans all holding winning tickets cheer him from their plastic-covered seats. They're swilling brown bottles of Corona Familiar that look absolutely gargantuan in their stubby little arms. Ritter gives them a polite nod and holds up his still-taped hand.

A properly grease-covered taco cart has been wheeled into the ballroom for concessions. Ritter makes his way over to the white-mustached old man and what looks to be his dark-haired granddaughter crewing the cart in their stained aprons.

"Cazadores, por favor," he requests.

The young woman, with a more-than-enthusiastic smile, serves him a shot of the tequila in a small plastic cup like the kind found atop liquid cold medicine bottles.

Ritter quickly knocks back the shot, grateful for the slow burn. He hands the plastic cup back to the girl.

"Uno mas."

She pours him another shot and Ritter makes it disappear just as quickly.

"Gracias," he says in an alcohol-constricted voice.

"You want something to eat, my friend?" the old man asks. "You don' wan' make yourself sick."

Ritter nods. "I'll have two, with carne asada."

He reaches into the pockets of his jeans for the sweaty wad of bills there.

"The shots are on me." A voice he'd recognize amidst the clamor of even the most raucous crowd.

Cindy is holding a Styrofoam cup in one hand and several betting tickets sorted among a shock of cash in the other. She walks up to Ritter with a big grin on her face, draining the remaining contents of the cup before tossing it. She peels off several bills and folds the rest, tucking them into the pocket of the fatigue jacket she's wearing.

"How'd you make out?" Ritter asks as Cindy pays the young woman for his order.

"Well, now, it went against all my instincts and all empirical evidence to bet on the white boy, but it did pay off."

The old man hands Ritter two corn-tortilla tacos on a paper plate, the fresh flank steak steaming under a bed of freshly chopped cilantro and onions. Ritter gratefully accepts the plate, dressing both tacos with salsa verde from a small plastic tub before picking up the first one and stuffing half of it into his mouth.

"Bronko has a gig for us," she tells him.

Ritter takes his time chewing and swallowing, his expression never changing. "You can handle it."

"See, now, nah, I can't. I'm not any kind of wizard."

"Neither am I."

"You're as close as we got, and we need you."

"I can't go back yet."

"Until when? You're forgiven? Until you've done enough penance? Is that what this is? The last time you did this shit was when you found out your old man kicked, and I figured, hey, he's working through some grief sprinkled with daddy issues, but this here—"

"What do you want from me, Cin? Seriously?"

"You didn't know what Allensworth had planned for the kid, all right? Gun to your brother's head, you made a damn decision. Who would've done different? Point 'em out to me."

"I didn't want to know. That's the truth. I couldn't undo what I did, so I closed my eyes and hoped it would all turn out ice cream and unicorn farts."

"And? Nobody died and you're not perfect. Now what? The rest of us are moving on here, Ritt."

"Lena isn't."

"She'll get over it!" Cindy insists. "Or she won't. Either way, she's not the only one there, man. We here, you're team. We all here because you came and got us and brought us here. That's on you, and you don't get to cut and run."

Ritter hurriedly finishes the last of his tacos and crumples up the paper plate, dunking it in a nearby commercial trash bin.

"I can't go back," he repeats after several long moments of silent thought. "But I'll back you up."

"How?" Cindy asks impatiently.

Ritter grins, just a little, and although it's an almost entirely rueful expression, it still does Cindy's heart good to see it.

"I happen to have a proxy available," he says.

HOME INVASION

Lena hasn't slept in her bedroom since returning home after the night of the two inaugurations. Without Darren, their apartment feels too much an empty, alien place to her. She almost wishes James would've stayed in Darren's room, and though she's neither asked nor offered, Lena supposes it's too hard for him, as well. She's had Nikki over several nights, and it helped, but Lena feels like she's exhausted that favor, even if her friend would never tell her so.

Lena has even found herself looking up Dorsky's contact in her phone half a dozen times, but even at three a.m., she's realized reopening that door is more trouble than it's worth.

Instead, she's nested in their living room, practically erecting a pillow and blanket fort around the second-hand couch they bought together with their first paychecks as line cooks in the city. Not that any of the comforts help; she can barely sleep, netting perhaps two solid hours on a good night. Every noise in the dark has her reaching for the retractable aluminum baton she keeps under the couch. Every dream waiting behind her eyelids is a nightmare.

If it weren't for binge-watching shows on Amazon Prime, she's not sure what the state of her sanity would be.

Lena stands in their kitchen after midnight, cracking fresh eggs into two ramekins, each lined with a strip of bacon. She's preheated their small oven. She doesn't whip or otherwise beat the eggs; merely sprinkles the top with dill, smoked paprika, and a pinch of pepper Jack cheese. After baking for ten minutes, she'll have two perfect bacon-wrapped eggs with golden, oozing yolks ready to be pierced.

Lena has just put the ramekins in the oven when she hears knocking at the front door.

It's not forceful or urgent. The knocking is entirely neighborly, except Lena isn't friendly with any of her neighbors and it's the middle of the night.

She hesitates and then reaches for a scaling knife from the gleaming set in a block on the countertop. She carefully tucks the blade inside the waistband of her pajama pants and covers the handle with the hem of the Old Navy tank top she's wearing.

Padding silently to the door in her bare feet, Lena stares through the peephole, and her breath immediately catches in her throat.

It's Allensworth.

Lena backs away from the door, mind racing.

"Miss Tarr," his weary voice addresses her through the door, "you've once again greatly overestimated the thickness of this portal. I can hear every step you take on the other side. Please do open up."

Lena sighs, looking down to double-check that the scaling knife she's secreted isn't visible. Satisfied, she steps forward and snaps the deadbolt, opening the door.

He's wearing the same black Adidas jogging suit he wore when delivering Darren's and her employment contracts for Sin du Jour, what seems like a lifetime ago.

His Rottweiler, Bruno, heels obediently by Allensworth's side.

"What do you want here?" she asks bluntly.

He laughs that mirthless, imitation laugh of his and shakes his head.

"I do, however, enjoy your forthrightness, Miss Tarr."

Lena doesn't say anything, simply waits.

"Inviting us in would be out of the question, I suppose," Allensworth says, glancing over her shoulder at the apartment beyond.

"You suppose right."

"Very well. Understandable. You've been through quite an ordeal as of late."

Lena feels equal amounts of disgust and rage twisting

into one pulsing knot in her gut. She has the deepest urge to quite literally slam the door in his smug, perpetually lying face.

Her next words drip like blood from her lips.

"Why . . . are . . . you . . . here?"

"I have news about Mr. Vargas."

That very benign sentence manages to break through the veil of red draped over Lena's world.

"Darren?"

Allensworth nods. "I've secured his release and I'd be quite happy to take you to him now if you'd like."

Lena begins to take a step forward, not even thinking, the very notion of seeing Darren again, alive and safe, overriding even her most taciturn sense of logic.

She stops.

"Why didn't you just bring him home?" she asks. "Why do I need to go to him?"

"I can do that, certainly. I'm on my way to sign him out now. I simply thought you'd want to come along, his being your very best of friends. That's all."

In that moment, Lena can't decide which enrages her more, the fact he's lying about Darren or that he really thinks she's a big enough moron to buy such an obvious lie.

"I don't believe a goddamn motherfucking word you say," Lena informs him. "I know you did that to him, whatever it was. I know you're making some kind of big power play. I know you think we're disposable. But you're just a wannabe dictator. And that's dictator with a little *dick*."

For the first time since laying eyes on the enigmatic figure, Lena sees Allensworth frown.

It's like watching the sun burn through a matte painting of false sky.

"Miss Tarr, it brings me far more pleasure than it should as an individual of my station to inform you that while you have been a stubborn pain in my ass from the day Byron hired you and your simpering little roommate, I am finally taking steps to excise that pain."

"So, I'm fired?"

Allensworth smiles, grandly and genuinely, revealing perfect ivory veneers and a hint of perhaps the pinkest gums Lena has ever seen not in a Hollywood starlet's mouth.

"My dear, sweet girl . . . beneath that ex-military swagger and Internet-feminist mouth, you really are just cloyingly stupid, aren't you?"

The strange arms that seize Lena's head and neck from behind are less like human limbs and more like winter tree logs wearing cashmere suit sleeves. Her throat is squeezed into the crook of a massive elbow while an equally massive hand presses the back of her head farther into the chokehold. Lena smells heavy musk and feels the wide body of a portly man pressing against her back. Her bare feet are no longer touching the floor.

Lena instinctively reaches up and claws at the man's arms and leather-gloved hands, but he's impossibly strong and it's as if his body is cemented in that position. She knows how to counter a rear naked chokehold, was taught countless times while grappling on a practice mat back in boot. There's no leverage she can gain, however, and no force she can exert to pry herself or her attacker's arms free.

Lena can feel her eyes bulging, bloodshot, out of their sockets. Her neck is already numb and her head full of cotton. Spittle runs over her lips unchecked. She can't breathe. Allensworth and Bruno are blurry shapes in her narrowing field of vision, but neither of them moves from where they're resting at the threshold of her door.

Lena knows in seconds, she'll lose consciousness. She forces her hands to abandon their futile ministrations, dropping them to her waist. She gropes at the band of her pajama bottoms until her fingers brush cool plastic. Her right hand closes around the grip of the scaling knife and pulls it free. Meanwhile, her other hand reaches up and grips the expensive material of the suit sleeve constricted around her neck.

Unable to look down, Lena uses the hold to guide her

trajectory as she jams the blade of the scaling knife into her attacker's arm, once, then twice, then over and over again in rapid succession. At first, he rocks her body from side to side, attempting to maintain his grip on her, but eventually a guttural scream fills her ear and the arm disappears from around her neck.

Lena drops to the floor, gasping for air until she finds herself hacking on it, feeling as though she might vomit. Ignoring the sensation, she commands her weakened, oxygen-deprived body to its knees, standing and turning to face her attacker.

The large man has backpedaled several feet, clutching his punctured arm. His jet-black Armani suit is impeccably tailored, as is the matching executioner's hood draped over his face, obscuring his head and neck completely save for two eyeholes. The irises beneath burn gold with flecks of crimson.

Lena extends the scaling knife and widens her stance. There's blood on the blade, on her hands and arms. There's blood on her chest and staining her tank top. She tries to ignore the macabre, triggering sight and coppery smell of it all.

The executioner rushes forward with a growl. With one swipe of his uninjured arm, he slaps the knife out of Lena's hand. Before she can react, that same arm reverses its trajectory and she's backhanded across the cheek and jaw with shocking power. Her legs seem to flee from beneath her and she crashes into the floor as if launched by a catapult, the entire left side of her face numb and stinging at the same time.

She feels his heavy footsteps advancing on her more than she hears or sees them in that moment. Shaking her head and blinking rapidly, Lena pushes away from the floor with her arms, bringing one knee under her for support. The other knee she draws close to her body, loading it like a spring. Lena focuses through her brain-addled haze and zeroes in on the executioner's right leg.

With all the power and momentum she can summon, Lena drives the heel of her left foot directly into the front of the man's knee. He might be large and thick through his limbs, but none of that padding is protecting his kneecap. The vulnerable area emits a sickening *pop* as the executioner's leg bends just slightly backward at an awkward angle. His advance halts, and he seems almost confused.

Then the report reaches the man's brain, and he begins to scream and scream.

Lena gets her feet back under her, still crouching low. In the midst of his agonized throes, the executioner reaches inside his suit jacket with his still-bleeding arm. Lena sees his hand emerge, coiled around the grips of a large semiautomatic pistol. Her eyes widening, she dives for his right leg, tackling him by his folded knee. The now one-legged giant topples, crying out even louder in pain and rage.

Lena quickly scrambles up his prone body, both hands reaching to secure the pistol on which he's managed to keep his grip. She wraps one hand around the barrel to secure the weapon's slide, her other hand working to pry the executioner's fingers loose. He's still stronger than her, maintaining his grip like a vice, at least until Lena jams her fingers into the puncture wounds of his arms and begins digging.

The executioner howls anew, and his hand unclenches just enough for Lena to pull the pistol from him. She quickly rolls away before he can reach for her, rising up to one knee several feet from where he lays.

The executioner sits up. Without thinking, Lena extends the pistol and pulls the trigger once. She doesn't even hear the shot that follows, only sees the man's hood burst like an overstuffed bag of feed. It's like pressing a deactivation button on an automaton; the man sits there on her floor, arms slack at his sides, head slumped towards his chest.

The bare threads of the hole left by the bullet in his executioner's hood are smoking.

Eventually, the man tips over onto his side, and when he hits the floor, it's like a spell has been broken. Lena blinks and leaps to her feet, turning toward her front door in panic.

Allensworth hasn't moved a muscle. He's still standing at her door in his absurd jogging suit, holding Bruno's leash patiently. The Rottweiler remains calmly heeled at his master's side, his tongue hanging out placidly.

Not even Allensworth's expression has changed.

Lena presses her palms together around the pistol's combat grips, sighting the bridge of Allensworth's nose through the weapon's crosshairs. Her finger tests the resistance of the trigger, finds it almost aching to be squeezed.

"Give me one reason I shouldn't blow your fucking head off right now," she says in a ragged voice.

There's blood in the corner of her mouth and the entire left side of her face is swollen and purple. Her body feels newborn in its pain and uncertainty. She feels like a completely different person in that moment, and it both frightens and compels her.

Allensworth sighs. "I can't think of a thing. But you aren't going to kill me, Miss Tarr."

"Ask your friend on my floor here about that."

"Oh, he wasn't a friend. He was barely a person. More like lunchmeat that received a massive upgrade. But I take your point. Also, it smells *delightful* in here. Is that bacon and eggs?"

Very slowly, and with his eyes never leaving hers, Allensworth crouches down and reaches for Bruno's collar.

The sights of Lena's pistol follow him the whole way.

He holds up one hand in a placating gesture while his other, still moving very slowly and meticulously, disconnects the end of the leash from the Rottweiler's collar.

Allensworth stands, lowering his hands and clasping them in front of him around Bruno's leash.

"If you don't think I'll shoot you, you better believe I'll cap your fucking dog," Lena assures him.

He nods. "Oh, I'm quite certain of that. But I'm afraid it's of little consequence. Bruno, *verwandeln!*"

The last word is spoken with a fury and a passion that seem completely alien on Allensworth's lips.

Bruno, meanwhile, leaps to all fours, his teeth bared in a growl as his entire body begins to shake, almost vibrating.

Lena shifts the pistol's sights from Allensworth to the canine and pulls the trigger.

The round strikes Bruno in the chest.

The Rottweiler doesn't seem to notice.

That's when she realizes Bruno has begun to grow. His fur and skin are stretching and forming new musculature right before her eyes. He rears back on two legs and she watches as all four of his limbs expand and begin to re-form into those of a biped. His snout and skull both double in size as well.

Allensworth carefully steps away from the door.

Lena fires two more times, both rounds hitting the creature center mass, neither shot having any more effect than the last. In fact, as Bruno continues to evolve, the slugs are pushed back through the holes they've torn in its body. Lena actually sees and hears the smashed bits of metal hit her floor.

She didn't think it possible after almost a year of working at Sin du Jour, but in that moment, she's more unnerved than she's ever been in her life.

When he apparently finishes, Bruno is well over six feet tall and must weigh four hundred pounds of thoroughly ripped muscle, claws, and fangs. If there were a Mr. Universe contest for canines, Bruno would've already been embroiled in a steroid scandal. He growls an entire baritone chorus of Rottweilers at her from the doorway.

Lena empties the pistol's entire magazine into the hellhound's body to no avail. She drops the spent weapon with a scream of frustration and anger and fear. It's too much, all of it, and it's crashing down atop her like a toxic wave.

When the beast finally leaps for her, Lena can't even command her legs to run.

HOME SECURITY

"You don't look much like Ritter," Bronko flatly states.

"Different moms," Marcus explains. "Mine was the pretty one."

Standing off to the side in Sin du Jour's lobby with Hara and Moon, Cindy can't help but let out a short laugh, cut even shorter by the diamond-hard eyes Bronko flashes her.

He looks back at Marcus. "Well. If Ritter says you can do the job, then you can do the job, I suppose."

"I promise if I make anything awful happen, it'll only happen to me," Marcus assures him, solemnly.

"Good 'nuff. Some kinda magical field protects this whole building here, part of the security system. In case of emergency, it automatically locks the place down. The problem is it's not under our direct control. It'd be real easy to use it to trap us all in here if the folks who *do* control it are of a mind. And they may be of a mind soon."

Marcus nods. "I also heard something about the entity that's been embedded in the system, some kind of dog?"

"Droopy Hound, from the Banjo Bear Gang," Moon says around a mouthful of mini powdered donuts he's eating from a family-sized bag. "That old cartoon from the sixties."

"Right. It must be some kind of spirit or demon taking the form of a cartoon character," Marcus reasons. "Which is a new one on me, but I've seen protection charms like it before. It's a simple matter of entrapping some nasty entity. Once it's in your thrall, you can program it like a computer to do or not do whatever you want. Not an easy process, but effective."

"Well, ideally, I'd like to put the whole system, including the damn cartoon dog, under our control. It'd be mighty useful. But worst case, I want it disabled so it can't be used against anyone in this building. And by *disabled* I mean shit-canned in totality beyond all repair."

"I understand," Marcus tells him, trying to stifle his amusement at Bronko's colorful language.

"I'll show 'im where to start," Cindy offers.

Bronko nods, and Cindy leads Marcus and Hara out of the lobby.

Moon lingers, fisting his oversized bag of sugary snacks.

"Aren't you goin' with 'em?" Bronko asks Moon.

He blinks up at Bronko incredulously. "To do what?"

"I dunno, maybe earn your keep around here?"

"I'm a specialist, boss," Moon insists in a mock-hurt tone.

"Well, when there's nothin' for you to eat, which near as I can figure is ninety percent of the time, you're as useless as tits on a bull."

Moon tries to summon feelings of offense, but they simply aren't there.

"Yeah, all right, fair," he says.

"I'll tell ya what, boy. Ryland ain't got nothin' on just now either. And near as I can tell, Cindy and Ritter find his company even less appealing than yours when the need arises. How about you go take some alchemist lessons from him? Your team could use the skill set in the field when you aren't eatin' the ass of a unicorn or whatever."

"You're serious?"

"Dead serious, less'n you're of a mind to take a pay cut."

Moon nearly chokes on his last powdered donut, coughing up crumbs. "I have . . . a . . . very expensive . . . video game . . . habit."

"Then hotfoot your ass to Ryland's trailer and tell him I said you both need to busy yourself in your off-hours here."

Moon recovers from the bout of donut asphyxia. He opens his mouth to protest, but Bronko's expression seems to polarize whatever words he had planned.

"All right," he relents. "I always hated school, but fine."

"Good boy," Bronko placates him.

After Moon has skulked off, sullen the whole way, Bronko takes out his phone and checks the time.

"Where the hell is Tarr?" he mutters to himself.

———————

The running pipes all around them sound like the veins of the world as Marcus and Cindy slog in rubber hip waders and fresh-air masks through three feet of mostly water and partly things they've silently agreed not to discuss in the moment.

" . . . so Ritter yells at me through the door, 'Marc, she's a banshee! Get out of there!' And I'm like, "Dude, we're kinda naked. I *know*! Go away!'"

Cindy laughs until she snorts, and at least fifty percent of the effort is based purely on the merit of Marcus's story.

He's walking two feet ahead of her in the narrow confines of the brick tunnel. They're at least a dozen feet beneath the lowest level of Sin du Jour. Marcus is guided by a small stone effigy of an anteater-like creature held in his right hand. The effigy's eyes are amber jewels blinking steadily in the dark. As they wade through the muck, he passes the anteater's snout along each wall, scanning the arch above, and even the foul viscous pooling fluid around their thighs.

It's the effigy that has led them into the bowels of the building, through a space that must've once been a cistern in the days before modern plumbing.

"It's hard as hell to be that funny and charming in a sewer tunnel," she says. "I give you a lot of credit."

"I notice you threw 'charming' in there."

"I should've tacked on 'perceptive' too, huh?"

Marcus abruptly halts. He's holding the anteater beside a patch of brick to his left, and its jeweled eyes have gone from blinking steadily to flashing rapidly.

"This must be it," Marcus says.

He feels along the section of wall, rapping his knuckles against it here and there experimentally. He returns the effigy to its surface, measuring the target area by the intensity of the eyes' flashing as he sweeps it, first from right to left, then up and down.

"Figure four feet across, starting here," he says, marking the area with a piece of bright blue chalk.

Cindy unzips a black OTS bag slung from her shoulder, removing a power drill with a long, thick, gleaming diamond bit. Firing it up, she begins piercing a dozen deep holes in the brick in a manhole-sized circular pattern. She finishes by drilling one extra hole in the dead center of the others she's fashioned.

"Is the blast going to go in or out?" Marcus asks, waving away the billowing clouds of brick dust.

"Neither," she answers with a grin, stashing the power drill.

Cindy removes a handful of cylindrical charges from her bag. She attaches wires to their ends and begins fitting one cylinder in each hole she's drilled, save that last hole in the center of the circle, which she leaves empty.

"Give it 'bout five feet clearance, just to be safe," she instructs him.

Marcus nods, and they both back away from her handiwork, Cindy moving down the tunnel and Marcus moving up until he's placed the appropriate amount of space between him and the blast zone.

"Clear!" she hollers a moment later before detonating the charges from a device in her bag.

It sounds as if the brick is being crunched between the jaws of some gargantuan steel-toothed creature. Dust spews in gunshot tendrils from the dozen holes Cindy drilled in the wall, filling the tunnel. There are shards of debris as well, but the wall itself remains mostly intact; rather than one large hole, she's simply blown a dozen small ones in the sewer.

Marcus slogs back towards the epicenter as the dust begins to waft up both ends of the tunnel. He watches

Cindy remove a two-foot aluminum rod from her bag, which she extends to four feet at the push of a button. She wipes one gloved hand over the perfectly round hole at the center of the blasted burrows she's made in the brick. She begins fitting the rod through that center hole.

When she's fed it most of the way, Cindy presses another button on the shaft. There's a metallic clanking sound on the other side of the wall.

"Help me," she says.

Marcus steps forward and the two of them grip the end of the rod tightly.

"Pull!" she commands.

Together they pry the manhole-sized section of bricks away from the rest of the wall, stepping aside and letting it drop into the mostly water, ignoring what splashes onto their clothing and the pungent stains left in its wake. Cindy retrieves her rod and collapses it, stashing it in the bag and trading it for a flashlight.

The space beyond the hole is a dry, cell-sized chamber. It is empty save for one object, a small stone crypt no bigger than an ice chest, sitting in the middle of the space. There are several arcane runes carved upon its heavy lid.

"That's it," Marcus proclaims. "That's the core."

"Are you sure?"

"Unless there's more than one conscripted supernatural entity bound down here."

"I mean, with this place, that's entirely possible."

"Trust me," Marcus says with a grin that reminds Cindy less of the real Ritter and more of one she's often fantasized about.

She hates the way it makes her feel, especially because she entirely enjoys the way it makes her feel.

Marcus begins climbing through the hole and into the chamber without another word. Cindy follows, watching him as he kneels beside the crypt and wipes away the dust over the runes, cleaning out the seams of the lid with his fingers and thumb.

"What happens now?" Cindy asks.

Marcus reaches inside his coveralls and produces what looks like a small ivory horn.

"It's just like pouring gas through a funnel," he assures her.

He pulls out an automatic knife with his other hand and deploys the blade. Marcus begins carving into the body of the horn. Cindy squints into the light of her aluminum torch. She sees that he's carving some of the same runes that mark the lid of the crypt into the white surface of the horn, along with other runes she doesn't recognize.

"I'm creating a conduit between the crypt here and our new vessel upstairs," he explains. "By making this horn an extension of the spell protecting the crypt, we'll be able to pop the lid, and instead of releasing whatever energy's inside, it'll be drawn into the horn and then funneled automatically to our vessel."

"Where'd you get this stuff?" Cindy asks. "The horn and the crypt-finder and whatnot."

"Ritter," Marcus answers tonelessly. "A purloined relic for every occasion, my brother has."

Marcus folds the blade back into his knife and returns it to his pocket.

"All right," he says. "Pop the lid."

Cindy nods, pulling out a stubby crowbar. She steps forward and crouches low, deftly fitting the flat end of the tool into the seam between the lid of the crypt and its body.

She hesitates.

"Now, you're sure about this here?" she asks him.

Marcus grins again. "Would you ask my brother that?"

"No, but I know him."

"Well, I'm here and he's not. How about you get to know me?"

"All right, then."

Cindy grips the crowbar tightly with both hands and presses her weight down atop it. The creaking of a thousand brittle bones fills the chamber and the lid gives way, just a crack, but it's enough to instantly and oppressively shift the air pressure in the small space and fill it with queer green light.

"Is this shit radioactive or something?" she asks in alarm.

Before Marcus can answer, the entire lid is blown clear of the crypt, shattering against the chamber ceiling and raining gravel down over them. An invisible force knocks Marcus off his haunches, the horn in his hands slamming him in the chest as he hits the ground.

Three stories above their heads, Hara is waiting in a secure room with a vintage 1966 Magnavox Magna-Color floor model television set procured by Marcus.

The stoic giant looks down as the antiquated piece of technology seems to leap half a foot from the ground. Once it settles, the TV begins visibly shaking as if an earthquake has seized the entire building. Hara and the rest of the room, however, are still as a graveyard. There's no power cord attached to the television set, and even if there were, there's no outlet in the disused storage room to welcome it.

Fortunately, Hara isn't the type to be unsettled, not even by a thing like the fifty-year-old TV's screen suddenly sparking back to life.

The sagging, ink-rendered features of Droopy Hound's face fill the screen. The animated character snaps his gaze from side to side, up and down, an expression of confusion and rage showing through his comical jowls. His head begins bouncing around the screen like a ping-pong ball in an old video game, but to no avail. A decidedly un-cartoon-like growl spits dust through the TV's speakers.

Droopy Hound eventually gives up, his image steady-ing into a wide shot of the moping dog standing in the middle of the screen in his trademark expressionless, sag-ging pose. He's wearing the uniform of an English bobby, no doubt a reference to some long-forgotten skit from his weekly cartoon show.

Several minutes later, there's a pounding at the steel door.

"Everything secure?" Cindy calls from the other side.

Rather than answer, Hara crosses the room and un-locks the heavy door from the inside, pulling it open for them.

Marcus and Cindy have ditched their hip waders, face masks, and other gear. Marcus stops short as soon as he spots Droopy waiting for them in the retro TV's screen. He slaps one hand across the other and lets out a tri-umphant holler.

"Hot damn! That's what I call one righteous magic hack, ladies and germs! It's Miller time!"

"Not yet, hot shot," Cindy reminds him.

"Right, yeah." Marcus clears his throat, assuming a more "responsible adult" stance. "But I mean, c'mon, you gotta admit we kicked a little ass. Big man, ya feel me?"

Hara just grunts.

"You feel me," Marcus maintains.

He walks over to the television set and hunkers down in front of the screen.

"For a moment, I was free," Droopy Hound says in his nasally, depressed voice.

"That's almost poetry," Marcus praises him. "And yeah, you were. Now you're going to do what we say."

Droopy's eyes look to the corners of the screen. "I remember these," he says. "I did my best work in them. Nobody believed children in those days. Humans were so wonderfully, willfully ignorant of reality. Not so anymore. I blame the Internet."

"So, that was your gig?" Marcus asks. "Take the form of a toon in a kiddy show, use it to siphon the essence of the kiddies?"

"Innocence was a heavily traded commodity, even in those days," Droopy assures him.

"Right. And was that a union gig, or were you working freelance?"

"I escaped from the bowels of hell before it became fashionable."

"I see. Were you human once? Some kind of Chester Molester or serial killer or both?"

"Who remembers anymore?" Droopy laments.

"So, Allensworth's people eventually caught up with you, and instead of returning you to hell, he stuck you in this building's protection charm."

"You're very sharp, sir."

Marcus looks up at Cindy, who shrugs.

"I'll tell you what," he says to the ensnared spirit. "I've got a new deal for you. I'm not going to tell you we'll set you free, because that ain't ever fuckin' happening while I'm alive. But if you go along with our little system reprogramming efforts here, I can promise you you'll finally taste blood again. And this time, it'll either be Allensworth or his people or both."

Droopy is quiet at first, but his normally forward-focused eyes turn up toward Marcus.

Eventually, his jowls spread in a menacing grin, so disturbing and unnatural to behold on the face of a cartoon designed and drawn to make children laugh.

"You're a bastard up to my own heart, sir."

Marcus laughs, shaking his head. He looks up at Cindy once more.

"Feeling me now?" he asks.

Cindy drops her head in an effort to hide the grin she can't suppress.

Marcus looks to Hara. "Big man?"

Hara lifts one frying-pan hand and shakes it in a "so-so" gesture.

It's Cindy's turn to laugh.

Marcus smiles. "I'll take it all day."

HOME VISIT

The front door to Lena and Darren's apartment is open when Bronko arrives, after hours and out of his executive chef whites.

He refuses to be alarmed, at least right away, despite the deep sense of dread Bronko feels bubbling just beneath the acidic surface in his guts. A lot of folks who are comfortable in their little secure old buildings leave their doors open, he reasons. The super could be making some late-night emergency repairs. Lena could've run across the hall for just a moment to a neighbor's place.

There are a million explanations, none of them even the least bit reassuring to him in that moment.

He steps inside.

Everything appears, at a first glance, to be in order. None of the furniture is disturbed. The television set is off, as are most of the lights. Bronko flicks the switch nearest to the front door, illuminating the foyer and pieces of the kitchenette and living room.

"Tarr? Are you home? Your damn door is open, girl!"

No answer.

Bronko wanders tentatively through the apartment, checking out the kitchen first, then walking over to the short hallway that leads to the bedrooms and bathroom. He flicks more light switches and briefly checks each room, finding nothing but made beds and dry showers. He returns to the living room, eyeing the couch, debating plunking down and waiting for someone to return or locking the door on his way out.

As he mulls those two options, Bronko's eyes lazily scan the foyer. They catch on a tiny flash of red glinting under the light beside the door. He moves around the couch and walks over to the spot, ignoring his aching joints and compressed fat parts as he crouches down to examine it. There's yellow in the red, and it feels chalky as he drags a thumbnail against the stain.

It's blood.

"Our mop-up crews aren't what they once were, I'm afraid," Allensworth says from the open doorway. "These new immigration laws are making it hard on everyone."

Bronko quickly stands, brain fizzing and fury in his eyes.

"What'd you do to my girl?" he demands.

"You see there, Byron? That's precisely the issue. You became far too attached to this young woman too quickly. I imagine you see something of your younger self in her, and a potential protégée. That's all understandable, but you've let it affect your judgment and, more importantly, your actions far too deeply. I simply can't have it."

Bronko takes a purposeful step towards him. "You're gonna tell me where she is, and she better be no worse off than when I last saw her."

Allensworth feigns hurt feelings. "Are you physically threatening me, Byron? Has it come to that between us?"

"I got no reason left not to tear you apart from mouth to asshole except that girl."

"Really?"

Allensworth reaches inside the blazer of his nondescript suit and removes a scroll capped at each end with ancient oak. He unfurls it with a flourish, revealing a two-foot document inked on papyrus in several languages, most of them deceased.

Both his and Bronko's signatures appear at the very bottom.

Bronko barely glances at the contract.

"You can give my damn soul to hell," he says in the darkest of voices. "I don't care anymore. But you ain't gettin' my people. Not a one of 'em."

"I'm not trotting out this document to remind you of your standing or obligations, Byron."

Allensworth reaches into his coat pocket with his other hand, and from it he produces a simple cocktail fork, holding it up for Bronko's inspection.

Bronko's eyes slit, confused, and he hesitates.

Allensworth, beatific smile on his face, presses the tines of the little fork to the surface of the contract and very gently drags it across the papyrus.

The invisible claws that seize Byron's innards in that moment reach a place inside him he's never before consciously felt. They squeeze there, suffocating and cutting at the same time. It's more painful and paralyzing than a heart attack, and occurring somewhere far deeper inside Byron. His knees fold and he collapses to the floor. His body is stiff and twisted, not even convulsing. He sputters and spittle flies from his lips, unable even to form sounds of agony.

What seem like a million years later, inhumanly strong hands begin lifting Bronko from the floor. His vision is all morning fog, but through it he registers Allensworth standing idly to the side, still smiling.

"I have a new job for you, Byron," his very distant voice says. "A brand-new kitchen for you to run. You're going to learn some much-needed lessons there, it is my sincere hope."

Bronko registers the words and their meaning, but he can't find the questions he knows he should be asking in his mind. There are no questions.

Eventually, there's nothing but darkness.

PART II

WAKING UP

SLACK

Moon's been knocking for five minutes at the door of Ryland's disabled RV permanently parked in Sin du Jour's loading dock. He's ready to give up when he begins to hear rattling inside the vehicle, followed by the shatter of glass and what sounds like a witch from a Shakespearean play with tuberculosis.

The door flies open so fast, Moon has to jump back to avoid catching it in the face.

"What manner of uncivilized, clearly primordial creature," Ryland demands, "thinks it proper to come calling at such a late hour of the evening?"

"It's the middle of the day, dude," Moon informs him.

Ryland pauses, squinting up at the afternoon sky.

"That would explain why the moon has been uncustomarily and quite, I may say, ineffectively replaced by the sun."

"Look," Moon begins, briskly, "Bronko told me to report to you for alchemist lessons. He said we both need to 'earn our keep,' whatever in the hell that means."

Ryland doesn't answer at first. Instead, he merely

stares at Moon as if he were speaking Chinese, despite the fact Ryland's Mandarin is quite adept.

"I understand nothing of what you've just said, young man."

Moon sighs. "Dude, I don't want to be here either, y'know? But Bronko's talkin' about cutting pay."

Ryland's bloodshot eyes widen as much as he is physically capable of doing in his condition, which means he can still be construed as squinting.

"Cutting pay?" he parrots back at Moon. "That's outrageous! Has he any idea of the overhead a finely tuned operation like mine carries with it? The insurance? The upkeep? The . . . the . . . my medicinal . . ."

He trails off, and Moon just watches him, half-fascinated and half-horrified.

"Cutting pay!" Ryland repeats in terror.

"Yeah, well . . . could you just teach me a few things?"

"Teach you . . . what, precisely?"

"I don't know! When you turned those demonic Santa's elves into stone, that was pretty badass. Teach me how to do that."

"I did no such thing!"

"I saw you!"

"You are clearly delusional!"

"We were attacked by a demonic North Pole and you turned half a dozen of those fuckin' things into lawn decorations. I was there."

"Child's babble!"

"Whatever, fine, let's just forget it."

"You wish to learn alchemy? Very well, here's all you need to know. It is a craft based around the concept of transmuting one thing from another. For instance, if I take this full bottle of fermented majesty," Ryland continues, holding up one of the cheap brands of wine he swills, "could you turn it into . . . let's say a pinch of the very fine marijuana you've clearly been smoking?"

Moon is caught off-guard. He's almost not sure he just heard what he clearly just heard.

"Are you saying . . ."

"I'm instituting your first lesson, and thus far, you're an abysmal pupil."

Moon hesitates, then reaches inside his pocket and produces a small cellophane fold of pungent green vegetation.

Ryland snatches it from him and pushes the wine into Moon's chest until he accepts it.

"There," Ryland proclaims. "You're an alchemist. Now, your next lesson will be turning this foliage into something smokable. Come inside."

Ryland disappears back into the RV with Moon's weed.

Moon, meanwhile, is left staring at the bottle in his

hands. He looks up into the dark confines of the recreational vehicle and grins.

"Okay, then," he says. "These are my kind of lessons."

THE NEXUS OF SPIDERS
AND SPIRITS

The girl's cries are angry winds echoing in a timeless canyon.

Little Dove is staring at a handwoven rug hung as a tapestry over the north wall of the small tract home's living room. The rug features colorful pictographs of four vaguely feminine figures. The two figures above have boxy heads and angular bodies with triangle hips, while the two below have been woven with larger diamond-shaped torsos, their legs reversed and red shapes stitched onto their bellies. They almost look like spiders with human heads.

"She's ready for you," White Horse informs his granddaughter.

Little Dove turns, watching him exit the room from which those cries continue to resound. She can smell the lingering spicy sting of burnt sage clinging to the air.

"What is this?" she asks the old man, waving at the rug.

"Spider Old-Woman, the spirit who taught our

women how to build looms and weave. Do you recognize her?"

Little Dove's face compacts in an annoyed expression. "Why would I?"

White Horse shrugs. "You're seeing now, aren't you?"

She frowns. "I'm not the fucking Ghost Whisperer, Pop."

"Watch your mouth in other people's houses, wiseass."

Little Dove seals her lips and gives him the finger.

White Horse ignores the obscene gesture. "It's time. She needs you in there."

"She needs *you*," Little Dove insists.

"You are ready for this."

White Horse steps aside and motions toward the open door to the bedroom.

His granddaughter stares resentfully up at his ancient, lined face, practically marching past him like an angry battalion.

The girl's name is Marta, she's nine years old, and her spirit is under siege by a darkness Little Dove can feel as she enters the room even if she can neither see nor understand it.

The little girl is wearing a simple blue dress and no shoes or socks. Her parents have used towels as soft restraints to bind Marta to her bed. Her small body thrashes against them as she continues to squeal and cry.

Her dark hair is pasted to the pillow with the same sweat that runs in heavy beads from her temples. Her eyes are affixed to the ceiling without actually seeing anything, and continually roll back into her head with her heaviest moans.

Little Dove's breath becomes shallow and sparse, and she can feel her heart throbbing against the wall of her chest. The blood in her veins feels electrified, the charge raising every tiny hair on her body.

"Pop!" she calls to White Horse. "Please come in here! Please? I can't—"

His voice booms from the living room. "Stop running your mouth for once in your short little life and focus on what's in front of you and around you!"

Little Dove swallows, looking anywhere except at the tormented girl tied to her small bed. There is another energy in the room with them. Little Dove feels it like the warmth of a single sun ray cutting through clouds swollen black and filling the sky. She senses intention, a benevolent purpose reaching through the membranes separating the Fourth World from the Earthly plane. Little Dove concentrates, tuning out everything, the sensory input of the room around her, the encroaching malice of that dark force infecting Marta's spirit, and even the myriad chaos of her own body and mind. She singles out that positive energy and exhales, doing everything she can to take it in and allow it to penetrate her.

"It's us!" she calls back to White Horse, a frantic relief in her voice. "It's our people! Her people! Her ancestors and family that've gone beyond! I can hear them!"

"They want to help the girl," her grandfather says. "They're *trying* to protect her, but they can't breach the veil alone. You have to be the conduit. You have to guide them from their world to ours and give them the power they need to use their will. Without you, they're wandering, lost, and the girl will be lost too."

"How do I guide them?"

"Dammit, you *know* how, girl!" White Horse insists. "You know everything you need to know. If you can feel them and hear them, then you can reach them! Stop letting your fear and doubt control you. Be who you are, what you are! Let yourself become the Hatałii you were born to be!"

She wants to argue with him, but Little Dove knows it's futile. She also knows it's not her grandfather's decision, not really. She agreed to come here, to learn from him, to explore whatever it is she's inherited that stirs within her, crackling and powerful like some caged beast growling to be free of its bars.

It all comes down to one question: does she want this?

Little Dove could go back to New York and become a baker under Nikki's tutelage. She could reject it all, leave everything Navajo behind in this squalid place White Horse has brought her to. She tells herself they're dying, all of them, and she doesn't have to become extinct with them. She won't be defined by something as random and out of her control as parentage or blood.

Marta's anguished cries pierce her thoughts and fill the space between Little Dove's temples. Little Dove thinks of her parents then, her mother and father, who succumbed to the despair they inherited in different ways but with the same fatal result. She remembers how much she wanted to help them both and how deeply it hurt when she found she could do nothing. Her mother cried like Marta, and those cries went unanswered until finally they ceased.

They are her people, all of them. She can no more leave them behind than she can sever her own arm and lay it in the dust.

Little Dove closes her eyes, her chin dropping to her chest as she raises her arms high, very much as she's watched her grandfather do before speaking in a voice that radiates with power beyond an infirm old man's possession. She can hear the voices of Marta's ancestors crying out even more fiercely now, answering the call of the girl's spirit in distress and under attack. Those voices and their energy are closer now but held back, restrained. Little Dove knows in that moment what the missing component is. She must let the darkness in, the malevolent energy filling this room as it spills out from Marta. She must open herself to it fully and use her own spirit to close the gap between the two opposing forces.

Little Dove opens her eyes and stars directly at Marta for the first time. She focuses her gaze, letting her eyes be the open windows that allow the malicious thing poisoning the girl's spirit to crawl inside of Little Dove as well. She feels the energy spark against her like a rusted plug in a faulty socket. She hears hundreds of young voices weeping in that darkness. They shed eternal tears there, trapped in the worst moment of their short lives. Little Dove realizes what malicious energy invades Marta's spirit. Teen suicide has reached epidemic levels among indigenous tribes, and this reservation is no exception. Every young life given over to that crushing fear and defeat and depression leaves a mark behind, a stain of the most negative spiritual energy. When enough such marks converge, they form a psychic chasm, a sucking pit of pure spite that spreads like a virus, seeking new spirits to corrupt.

Little Dove begins chanting, repeating the words learned from her grandfather. She becomes a nexus point in that moment, a bridge between Marta's ancestral spirits and the blind, pure malevolence assaulting the girl. That spiritual energy, the sum of a thousand generations, rushes over the bridge to meet the darkness like a band of warriors pouring into the valley of their enemies. The two forces clash and the light pierces the malevolent pitch, overtaking it as light is forever destined to do when introduced to the darkness.

Little Dove loses all sense of time, her surroundings, and even reality. In the next moment, she finds herself perched on her hands and knees against the floor, gasping for fresh air. Feet and legs shuffle past her as Marta's parents rush to the girl's side, crying and cooing and praising as they untie her. The girl is no longer crying or thrashing. Little Dove raises her head to see Marta fast asleep in her mother's arms, her slumbering face serene and untroubled.

White Horse groans as he forces his brittle aging bones to bend, crouching beside her on the floor. He gently strokes the hair back from Little Dove's face to find hot tears stinging her cheeks.

"How does it feel to be a medicine woman?" he asks.

She doesn't answer him. There's no feeling of victory. Her mind is with the lost children whose weeping she will hear in her dreams for years to come.

"You can't save everybody," he says, as if he can read her thoughts. "I suppose that's what makes saving the ones you can even more important."

Little Dove makes a sound that might've been a laugh

under any other circumstance.

"When did you stop being an asshole, Pop?"

White Horse smiles. "Dunno. I guess you did what five wives couldn't."

"What's that?" Little Dove asks.

"You made me finally grow up," he says.

BRING HITHER THE FATTED CALF, AND . . .

Lena smells chocolate and freshly baked pastry dough.

She's aware of salivating before she's truly awake. Lena smacks and licks at her lips, her eyes opening to soft artificial lighting. She's lying on a military-style cot wedged into a corner. The walls are metallic with chipped white paint. Blinking and looking around her, she sees she's been sleeping in a wide stall with no door. There's a sink and a toilet affixed to the adjacent wall. Strangely, there are several thick steel rods hinged between the toilet and the floor, as if they're propping it up or reinforcing it.

Another smell stings her nostrils with a sharp, piney scent. It's sawdust; she can see the floor is thickly seasoned with the stuff.

Lena realizes how unusually wide the cot is when she has to roll twice to reach the edge. It could sleep two more of her easily. She swings her legs over the side and sits up, a dull pain between her ears. She's no longer wearing the bloodstained tank top and pajama pants in which she was abducted. They've dressed her in black work pants, matching boots, and a black chef's smock.

She stands, her head throbbing just slightly, and crosses over to the stall's sink, above which is a mirror that seems as unnaturally wide as the cot. There's a small cut at the corner of her mouth, and much of her left cheek is purple and blue. Other than that, Lena appears unscathed.

She touches the left breast of her smock. There's a logo there, not Sin du Jour's. There are no words, only the black-against-yellow shape of a palm tree, its trunk crossed with a wicked-looking axe, like something used by a medieval executioner.

Lena has no idea what it means.

She pokes her head out of the stall. There are at least twenty more lined up on either side of the room. They all seem empty right now. There are no doors at either end of the two rows, just wide, open archways leading out. Lena realizes those delicious dessert smells are emanating from beyond one of the arches.

Seeing no other alternative, she follows her nose.

It's like walking into a real-life wing of Willy Wonka's factory. The space is the size of a warehouse, and virtually all of it is filled with desserts, brightly colored confectionery creations straight out of a magazine and industrial-sized parcels of prepackaged treats. Wheels of cheese the size of big rig tires are stacked five high. There is a literal mountain of donuts piled into a perfect twenty-five-foot peak inside what looks like an indoor pool. Lena peers over the side and finds the bottom of the donut mountain sitting in what must be a hundred gallons of viscous white frosting.

She walks past library-tall shelves of different cake slices behind small glass doors. In the distance she can see a chocolate fountain as large and opulent as any fountain in the Vatican.

Only it's chocolate.

Above the burbling of the fountain, Lena begins to register a new sound, the first sign of life she's encountered thus far in this bizarre place. Lena hears the wet, gnashing chorus of animals, dozens of animals, feeding all in a row. It's interspersed with sounds of pleasure that are almost human. They must be feeding all of this crap to pigs or cows or some kind of barnyard life, although why she can't fathom.

Lena follows the sound to its source. She rounds several dozen side-by-side racks of chicken and waffles under what appears to be a system of garden sprinklers intermittently spritzing syrup instead of water.

It's not animals. Lena stares at the mountainous backs of six morbidly obese men and women. They're sitting shoulder to shoulder on oversized stools in front of a long table, gorging themselves on every manner of confection this fantasyland of desserts has to offer. They all wear simple beige coveralls with bibs tied around their bulging necks. Each one of their heads has been shaved bald, giving them the appearance of gargantuan babies.

Lena has to battle against the urge to retch. She averts her eyes from the obscene binging. Attendants stand at each end of the table. They're dressed like busboys, wearing the same logo with which Lena woke up marked. Gleaming black plastic helmets cover their face and heads. The attached masks are molded with nondescript facial features, giving them the aspect of automatons.

She watches the pair work. One attendant is responsible for constantly loading fresh offerings onto the table in front of the feasters. The other attendant uses a long industrial broom to pull and sweep empty dishes, wrappers, and food debris into a large trash bin.

It is possibly the most revolting sight she's ever witnessed.

"Miss Tarr! You've rejoined us! Excellent."

The voice, feminine and welcoming without an ounce of genuine warmth, is vaguely familiar to Lena. She turns around, practically blinded by the shocking pastel green of the woman's finely tailored skirt suit. The speaker is wearing matching eyeglass rims, a shock of the same color running through the otherwise dark hair tied up in a bun atop her head. Her only accessory not matching her suit, in fact, is the crimson leather attaché case held at her side.

It's Luciana Monrovio, Allensworth's succubus toady, wearing an empty smile Lena immediately wants to punch off her face.

"Where the fuck am I?" Lena asks.

Something sinister touches that plastic, prepackaged smile of Monrovio's.

"Welcome to Gluttony Bay."

GET MORE

"Welcome back to Gluttony Bay, sir!" the maître d' greets Allensworth warmly. "It's been far too long!"

"I wholeheartedly agree, Alfonse. How have you been?"

"Quite well, quite well!"

Alfonse is resplendent in tuxedo and tails, spotless white gloves covering his hands. He resembles any high-end host in the restaurant world, save for the silken executioner's hood draped over his head and face. It's jet-black with Gluttony Bay's logo emblazoned on the forehead, the stitched eyeholes threaded with the same yellow.

"Are you dining this evening, sir?" he asks Allensworth.

"Not at the moment. I have a surprise to present to our guests."

Alfonse clasps his gloved hands in front of his chest, his back arching impossibly deep in elation.

"That is fabulous! Your surprises are the stuff of legend."

"May I address the diners?"

"But of course!"

Alfonse escorts Allensworth into the opulence of the main dining room. The floor is yellow-and-black marble. The ceiling is overwrought with a twenty-four-karat gold and emerald palm tree forest. Many of the tables are arranged family style, long and draped in yellow and black linen, but there are also private booths lining the walls. The booths are far more private than your standard lovers' nooks, coming complete with closing doors on each. The servers all wear the same molded plastic face masks and helmets; none of the staff, in fact, reveal their faces.

The clientele is largely demons of the upstart Vig'nerash clan, all of them decked out in their best Hugo Boss. There's also a large group of squat, albino-white ghouls with their saggy, cottage-cheese faces. They wear funereal suits and all seem to have comically obvious wigs atop their heads. Very few humans patronize the place.

Allensworth strolls to the middle of the tables, addressing the restaurant at large. "Excuse me, gentlefolk; may I have the attention of the dining room for a moment?"

All heads turn toward him, and all seem to recognize Allensworth on sight.

"We greatly appreciate our guests here, and in our continued efforts to show it, I have a surprise for the loyal diners of Gluttony Bay, something to enhance what I hope you all agree is already the ultimate dining experience."

The kitchen doors are flung open and two attendants wheel out a towering gift-wrapped package the size of a phone booth to the delight and anticipation of the crowd. They bring the giant present to a rest a few feet from where Allensworth stands.

"My fellow Gluttony Bay patrons, it is my deepest pleasure to present to you your very special guest chef for the weekend. You've no doubt eaten in his restaurants and many of you will remember him from his game-changing weekly cooking program, *The Double-Cross Ranch Chuck Wagon*, and his winning season of *Survivor: Celebrity Chef Edition*. I give you . . . Bronko Luck!"

The attendants tear the wrapping away from the front of the package and pull open the door of the crate beneath.

Bronko stumbles out into the light of the restaurant, confused and shielding his eyes with one hand. He's wearing the same black boots, pants, and smock as those in which Lena awoke, only his has full-length sleeves and more decoration, befitting an executive chef.

The crowd cheers riotously. Bronko lowers his hand as his eyes adjust, scanning his surroundings.

"Byron!" Allensworth greets him over the bedlam. "Welcome back!"

He strides forward and slips an arm around Bronko's wide shoulders, gesturing grandly to the approval and further cheering of the crowd.

"What is this?" Bronko asks him.

"Think of it as a field trip," Allensworth answers, for Bronko's ears only. "An educational one. Now, don't make a scene. These are all important people, human and non. Think of your own staff you expressed such concern for. Their fate is tied to yours here."

Bronko's head is spinning, but Allensworth's words register plainly all the same.

The maître d' approaches them, applauding animatedly.

"Alfonse, meet Chef Bronko Luck!" Allensworth bids him.

"It is such an honor to have you here, Chef," the hooded man praises Bronko. "I cannot even imagine the interpretations of our cuisine you will offer! It is so exciting!"

Allensworth claps Bronko between the shoulders several times and steps away. "I'll leave you in Alfonse's capable hands for now, Byron. I have other business to attend to here, but I promise we will reconvene soon. Understood?"

Bronko nods dumbly, unsure of what else to do in that moment.

Satisfied, Allensworth turns and exits the dining room, leaving him alone with the maître d'.

"Are you all right, Chef?" Alfonse asks. "You seem a bit livid. You are feeling well, I hope?"

Bronko does his best to shake it off, remembering what Allensworth said about his staff.

"No, I'm . . . I'm good. I'm sorry. I don't like being packed in giant birthday boxes."

"Of course! Who does, after all?"

Alfonse giggles beneath his hood, and there's something very disturbing about the combination.

"Um . . . tell me, Alfonse, what kind of restaurant is—"

Bronko trails off. He stares out through the panoramic windows of the restaurant at the blue and grey waters of the bay. It is undeniably beautiful, but he quickly realizes it's not the only feature the view offers the restaurant's patrons.

Across the bay Bronko sees many tall fences crowned with barbed wire. He sees tall guard towers with blacked-out windows.

Finally, he sees a large sign enblazoned with military insignia erected in front of a grey stone acropolis.

CAMP DELTA, it proclaims in bold black block letters.

His mind offers him no alternate explanation. He knows exactly where he is.

"Guantanamo," Bronko barely manages to force past

his lips. "That . . . that is fucking Guantanamo Bay out there."

"But of course, Chef!" Alfonse happily confirms. "Where else would we establish such a rarified fine-dining experience as this?"

Bronko's mind is racing, and the track doesn't lead anywhere that's not utterly horrific.

"I'm guessin' y'all don't serve Cuban food here," he says quietly, a timbre of pure dread underscoring his voice.

"Rarely, Chef," Alfonse informs him casually. "The menu is largely Middle Eastern. We also do wonderful Chinese, and even the occasional Russian. Now, I don't mean *fusion*, you understand."

The hooded maître d' pats Bronko's arm and laughs heartily at that, as if he's made an everyday joke.

Bronko doesn't laugh. His flesh has begun to crawl and tremble uncontrollably beneath his new executive chef uniform. He looks from the chuckling maître d' to a nearby table, where a foursome of Vig'nerash demons is currently being served by one of the restaurant's faceless waiters.

A covered platter is placed on the table between them. Something in Bronko screams at him to look away, while another voice, a much more jaded and calm voice, not unlike Allensworth's, tells him he already knows what he's about to see, and there's no point in denying it.

The masked waiter lifts the stainless steel lid from the platter with a flourish.

In the next moment, Bronko finds himself staring into the placid, glazed eyes of a severed human head. It's resting on a bed of butter lettuce leaves and garnished with spirals of lemon slices and mint sprigs. What appear to be roasted chestnuts fill the deceased man's mouth.

"Shall I show you the kitchen, Chef?" Alfonse offers.

Bronko's mouth feels full of cotton. The world around him, every sight and sound, seems to have slowed. He has to struggle to move his gaze from the maître d' and the entirely ordinary eyes beneath his hood to the nearest sharp knife, resting atop a napkin on a nearby table.

He can see himself taking up that knife and scoring Alfonse like the fatty layer of a roast. He also knows, beneath the shock and terror he's experiencing, how irrational and ultimately self-destructive a course of action that would be.

"I'd like . . . to freshen up first," Bronko manages to say.

"Oh, of course, Chef!" Alfonse sounds absolutely appalled "How atrocious of me! You've traveled so far. I'll have you escorted to your quarters immediately!"

"Thank you," Bronko hears himself tell the odious little man.

He waits, trying not to see what's happening at every

table around him, trying not to see what else is wheeled out of that kitchen.

Later, he'll tell himself he succeeded, and most nights, he'll even be able to believe that lie.

ONE WILL NOT COME BACK

In approximately twenty minutes, Jett will sincerely wish that walking in on Nikki and Dorsky making out in Sin du Jour's pastry kitchen was the most noteworthy and most disturbing news of the day.

But right now, she's still en route to the small haven of baking ovens perpetually smelling of maddeningly fresh dough, and it's Dorsky surprising Nikki with his presence.

"You alone back here?" he asks, popping his head around the side of the kitchen's open arch.

Nikki nearly drops the tray of cherry amaretto cookies she's holding in hands covered by oven mitts shaped like starfish. She places it down atop one of her stainless steel prep stations and shakes the gloves loose like a hockey player preparing for a brawl. She removes the buds from her ears. The faint strains of a Muse song can be heard.

"What did you say?" she asks.

"I was asking if you're alone back here."

"Just me and the live yeast," Nikki says with an uncertain smile.

"No, I just meant . . . I guess I expected to find Lena back here power-drinking wine."

"Oh. She didn't come in today, I don't think."

Dorsky walks over to her, eyeing the cookies she's just taken out of the oven with interest.

"Have one if you want," she bids him. "I'm baking them to send Mr. Mirabel's family."

"That's cool of you."

Dorsky picks up a cookie and bites into it. "Jesus, how do you do this?" he asks, almost dreamily.

Nikki grins. "Natural talent."

He quickly polishes off the rest of the treat. "Listen, I haven't really . . . I guess I just wanted to make sure you were okay. We haven't really talked since the inauguration."

"Do we . . . and I'm not trying to be a dick here, because I see you're trying to be nice . . . but do we 'talk,' Tag?"

At first, Dorsky looks taken aback by that question, but in the end, he realizes it's a fair point, and he nods.

"All right, yeah. But we used to, right? I mean, at least a little. And like I said, I was worried about you."

"You didn't say it, actually," Nikki points out quietly.

Dorsky looks directly into her eyes, his expression soft on her. "I was worried about you," he says.

Nikki feels that thing happening inside of her that she

promised herself after the incident with Dorsky and the succubus would never happen again.

She's also starkly aware of how close he's standing to her.

"I'm doing good," she tells him. "I promise."

Dorsky nods. "That's good. Like I said—"

"You were worried. And you did say it. That time."

Somewhere between some of those words, and Nikki isn't even sure which, Dorsky begins kissing her, and when she's finished with her last sentence, she finds she's kissing him back. His hands close against her ample hips and half-urge, half-lift her up onto the countertop behind her.

Jett clears her throat delicately.

When that doesn't pierce their lust bubble, she clears her throat like a forty-year-old trucker who smokes five packs a day.

Nikki snaps back to reality with a start, pushing Dorsky away and blinking rapidly.

"Oh my god no please why no," she babbles as she spots Jett watching them. "This is so incredibly absolutely totally not what it even kind of looks like I swear I swear I swear . . ."

"It's kind of what it looks like," Dorsky insists.

Nikki wedges a knee between them and wriggles her foot against his lower abdomen, using it to shove the towering sous chef away from her. She slides off the counter and begins frantically straightening and smoothing her chef's smock.

"Listen, Jett—" she begins.

"Nikki, it is your kitchen, it is your business," Jett assures her. "I apologize for interrupting."

"You were not interrupting anything!" Nikki insists again.

"Kinda were," Dorsky reiterates, only to be punched in the shoulder.

"Do either of you know where Byron is?" Jett asks. "I haven't seen him all day, and I can't raise him on any of his numbers."

Nikki frowns in immediate concern. "No, Jett, I haven't seen Chef Luck since yesterday."

Dorsky shrugs. "Chef probably needed some personal time. Can't blame him, things being the way they have lately."

"It's not like him not to check in with me, Tag, *especially* with things being the way they are lately."

"You know, Lena didn't come in yesterday, and she's not here today, either," Nikki points out. "I tried calling her last night, but she didn't pick up. She hasn't been sleeping since . . . well, since Darren's been gone, so I'd hoped she finally just crashed."

It's Jett's turn to frown in concern. "I do not care for this pattern."

"They're both cool, I'm sure," Dorsky insists. "We could all use some time off."

"I hope you're right," Nikki says.

"Why don't you ask ol' Boosh where they're at?" Dorsky suggests, referring to Boosha, Sin du Jour's resident sage and arcane food taste tester. "That old broad always seems to know what's happening or has happened or, like, is going to happen. It's freaky."

Jett furrows her brow in contemplation. "That . . . is actually a surprisingly useful and helpful suggestion, especially coming from you. Thank you, Tag."

Dorsky looks back at Nikki and grins as he says, pointedly, "I'm growing as a person. It's my new thing."

Nikki rolls her eyes, but she's also smiling.

"Whatever, dude."

"Well, then," Jett says, awkwardly clapping her hands in front of her. "I'll leave the two of you to your . . . work."

She turns on her stiletto heel and clacks away from the pastry kitchen's open arch.

Jett reappears a moment later.

"I am so sorry for this," she says, "but I just have to say it. Please, *please* do not have intercourse in this kitchen. It is so incredibly unsanitary, but more than that, the health code violations and liability issues alone—"

"Jett!" Nikki exclaims, her embarrassment verging on outright horror.

"Lady, you keep zombies pent up in the storeroom," Dorsky reminds her.

Jett's eye widen in offense. "I employ a *living-impaired* workforce, Tag, and they are perfectly sterile, I assure you."

"Jett, I love you, but please go away now," Nikki implores.

"Right, yes," Jett says reproachfully. "I apologize. I am just . . . me, I guess. Have a good day."

She leaves them and the pastry kitchen behind, her six-inch Louboutin heels carrying her ever precariously but fashionably through the corridors of Sin du Jour until she reaches Boosha's ramshackle, cluttered apothecary/library. She finds the door open, as it always is. She also finds the not-quite-human-yet-not-quite-distinctly-anything-else woman inside, as Boosha always is.

She's hunkered over her lectern, examining the steadily crumbling pages of one of her ancient volumes. Her cloud of white hair obscures most of her green-tinted face.

"May I enter, Boosha?"

"Of course, fancy lady," Boosha answers in her thoroughly unrecognizable accent.

Jett clacks a few feet inside the door, frankly terrified to disturb anything in the overstuffed closet of a room lest she cause an avalanche.

"Have you seen Byron?" she asks. "He hasn't come in today, and he always lets me know when he'll be absent during office hours."

"Bronko gone," Boosha states plainly.

"I am aware of that, Boosha," Jett replies patiently. "Is he at home, do you know?"

Boosha shakes her head. "Bronko gone-gone, far away. Not here no more."

Jett blinks in surprise, her mind taking a moment to catch up to the implications of the old woman's words.

"Boosha . . . *where* has he gone?"

"Taken," Boosha corrects her. "Cannot say where or by who. Do not know."

Jett's voice rises in shock and alarm. "Bronko's been *taken*?"

Boosha nods emphatically, head still buried in her ancient tome.

"Lena, too," she confirms.

"Wait . . . wait . . . Bronko *and* Lena have been taken? If that's true, why didn't you tell anyone?"

"I tell you," Boosha reminds her impatiently.

"Because I came in here and asked! Why didn't you come get someone? Why aren't you more concerned?"

Boosha waves a hand at her. "They will be back."

"They will?" Jett asks, no less confused.

"Yes."

"I . . . okay, then. Fine. Thank you."

She turns and walks back out through the open door.

"One will not," Boosha mutters.

Jett stops, turning around. She clacks her heels back inside the apothecary.

"What did you say, Boosha?"

"They will be back, Bronko and Lena, but one will not come back."

"Which . . . *one*, Boosha?" Jett asks. Then, more urgently: "Do you know who? Who are you talking about? Who won't be back?"

Boosha again shakes her head emphatically. "Cannot say. Only know one will not come back."

Something in those words chills Jett to her ordinarily unshakeable core.

This time when she turns to leave, Jett reaches down and yanks off both of her heels so that she can run.

THE FUTURE IN THIRTY MINUTES
OR LESS

Ritter spots the dried blood spatter on the floor within five seconds of entering Lena and Darren's apartment.

"Is it hers?" Marcus asks, standing over Ritter, who is crouching down to examine the stain.

"How could I possibly know that?" he fires back, irritated in that way only his brother can make him.

"The apartment's clear!" Cindy announces, emerging from the hallway a moment later and securing her tactical tomahawk to its tie-down rig on her hip.

Hara follows her past the living room to join the brothers in the foyer. Moon is unusually absent from the group, having told them, shockingly, he had alchemy lessons to attend with Ryland.

"No signs of a struggle," Cindy says. "Not to sound all beat - cop - at - the - beginning - of - a - *Law - and - Order -* episode and whatnot."

"Somebody cleaned up after a struggle," Ritter insists. "They just missed a spot. Bronko was here, too."

"How do you know that?" Marcus asks.

"I can still smell his aftershave. It's faint, but it's here next to the blood, like he was rolling around on the floor."

"You would've made a helluva detective, my brother. So, what, they were taken together, or . . ."

"No," Cindy says to Marcus. "Jett told me Lena didn't come in yesterday and Bronko was all worried. Then Bronko didn't come in today, and Jett or nobody can get ahold of him. That's when I called y'all."

Marcus nods, seeing the whole picture now. "So, Bronko came looking for her, and whoever or whatever took this Lena chick took him, too."

"Don't talk about her like she's a stranger," Ritter instructs him.

"Didn't mean anything by it, bro. What's our next move?"

Cindy's expression is grim. "They could be anywhere in the fucking world by now, if they're even alive. We got nothin.'"

Hara grunts his agreement.

Ritter thinks for a moment and then takes out his phone. "Who's got cash on them?"

"A few bucks," Cindy says.

Hara removes a gold horse-head money clip from his pocket and holds it up. There's a thick fold of bills held in the horse's jaw.

Marcus shrugs. "I'm tapped, bro."

"Shocking."

"What are you doing?" Cindy asks as he begins dialing.

"I'm ordering a pizza," Ritter answers in that bland way of his that makes it impossible to discern whether he's joking or not.

Her eyes widen. "This seem like the time to eat to you?"

"I'm hungry," Marcus offers.

"Just wait," Ritter bids them, listening to the other end of the line ring.

"Yeah," he says to whoever answers. "I'd like to order the deluxe special."

He gives them Lena and Darren's address and ends the call. Twenty-eight minutes and one in-depth discussion between Cindy and Marcus about how much better *The Matrix* would've been if Brandon Lee had lived to star in it later, there's a knock at the door and Ritter answers it. The rest of them, particularly Cindy, are eager to see who has come calling at his request, crowding in front of the couch in the living room for a clear view.

If anyone besides Ritter was expecting to see a clown standing in the hallway holding a pizza box, his painted face pierced dozens of times through the ears and nose with silver rings and studs, none of them shows it.

In fact, even Hara, who generally has one expression

for all occasions, looks confused.

The deliveryman's face is white with blue and grey diamond shapes over his eyes and mouth, clashing with his classically bulbous red rubber nose, although it does match his oversized clown shoes. A spiky black wig covers his head, and his clown suit is also gleaming silver with diamond-blue ruffle and highlights.

The pizza box propped up on his white-gloved hand bears the logo of a Papa Augie's Pizzeria, which is a stopwatch in the shape of a pizza pie.

"Hey, Tommy," Ritter greets the man.

"Hey, Ritt. You order a deluxe special?"

"I did, yeah."

When he speaks, they can all see that the delivery clown's teeth have been filed into sharp, wicked-looking fangs.

"Come on in," Ritter bids him.

Tommy walks inside, his banana boat shoes smacking loudly against the hardwood floors. He drops the pizza box none too gently down on the dining table near the kitchenette. Pulling out a chair, he plops down on it tiredly and leans back with a sigh.

"Long day?" Ritter asks him.

"Dude, you don't even know. Pop's slowing down. My brother up and quit the business, got himself a fucking nine hundred number or something. It's hard times for divining in Italian-inspired food items."

"Well, it was a rarified trade to begin with," Ritter observes, his patience wearing thin.

"True dat," Tommy begrudgingly admits, nodding. "So, what do you need? A reading? Past? Future?"

"Present. I need a locate."

"Ah, of course!" Tommy laughs. "Everybody is so damn practical these days. No nuance in our customer base, you know? No appreciation of what's come before or what's to come. It's all 'Find my deadbeat husband.' 'Tell me if my girlfriend's at that motherfucker Andre's house again.' I'll tell ya, man—"

"Tommy, seriously," Ritter cuts him off.

"Right. Sorry. What do you have?"

Ritter takes out the vial and holds its red flecks up to the light. "Blood."

"Groovy."

Tommy leans across the table and pulls the pizza box toward him. Rubbing the gloved fingertips of his hands together, he carefully flips open the lid, revealing the contents beneath.

They all lean over the table, and Cindy immediately turns away in horror, throwing an arm across her face. Marcus's mouth fills with air as if he may vomit, and even Hara is forced to frown.

Rather than pepperoni or sausage or mushrooms, the

"pizza" is topped with a healthy amount of tiny eyeballs, insects of half a dozen varieties, dead leaves, and small, fetid organs.

"What is that, a sushi pizza?" Cindy asks in open disgust.

"I could totally go for sushi," Marcus says.

"It's our deluxe divining pie," Tommy informs them. "Give me the blood."

Ritter hands him the vial, and Tommy uncaps it, holding it directly above the center of the "pizza."

Cindy is dubious and completely uninterested in hiding it. "You're telling us sprinkling some dried blood on that culinary monstrosity is going to let you find our friend anywhere in the world?"

"This world, other worlds, yeah," Tommy answers without emotion.

"Bullshit," Cindy says.

Tommy looks up at her, wearily. "Lady, who's the psychic pizza-delivering clown here, you or me?"

Cindy is suddenly at a loss.

"I . . . I mean, you are, clearly" is all she can say to that.

"Thank you."

Ritter quickly stifles a small smile, shaking his head just so.

Tommy gently sprinkles the dried blood flakes on the pizza. As soon as the first speck touches the surface of the pie, the entire circular object seems to spring to life. The cheese begins bubbling. The inert bugs begin crawling. The organs pulse anew. Even the eyes seem to focus.

It is very, very disturbing.

Tommy waits while the rest of them try not to look away. Both Cindy and Marcus fail.

Less than a minute later, the activity ceases, but those seconds will last a lifetime for most.

"All righty, then," Tommy says, producing a pizza cutter from the pocket of his suit.

"Wait! You're not gonna—" Cindy begins, and stops as he slices into the pie.

"Respect the psychic pizza-delivering clown suit, lady," Tommy reiterates, carving out a wedge of divining pizza.

He takes up the slice in his gloved hand and flashes them all a smile full of spears.

"Kids, don't try this at home," he warns, and bites off a large section of the slice.

Cindy nearly retches watching him chew, but what happens in the next moment thankfully distracts her. Tommy's body seizes, going stiff as a board against the chair. His eyes roll back in his painted face. The whites of them turn into black pools.

"Is he cool?" Marcus asks.

Ritter only nods.

The episode lasts for thirty more seconds, and when Tommy's body unlocks and the color returns to his eyes, he begins hacking up bits of pizza.

Amidst the convulsions, he groans a series of numbers.

"What's that?" Cindy asks.

Ritter is already typing the numbers into his phone. "Latitude and longitude," he explains.

They all wait, watching Ritter.

In the next moment, his expression becomes as dark as any of them has ever seen.

"Where?" Marcus asks.

Instead of answering, Ritter looks down at Tommy. "Was it her? A girl? A young woman, mid-twenties, dark hair?"

Tommy nods.

"And you're sure?" he asks, although it's clear he doesn't want Tommy to be sure.

The psychic clown nods again. "You called me, dude."

Cindy is ready to start yelling. "Ritter, where is she?"

"Cuba," he says. "Guantanamo."

"Like . . . Guantanamo-Guantanamo?" Cindy asks.

"Yeah."

"Holy shit," Marcus says. "But that means—"

"Gluttony Bay," Ritter finishes for him. "It has to be."

Cindy remains lost. "What in *the* hell is Gluttony Bay?"

"I'll explain on the way, but we need to go now," Ritter tells her.

"Yo!" Tommy interrupts. "Somebody owes me three grand, plus tip."

"Three fucking grand?" Cindy practically explodes.

"Plus tip," Tommy confirms.

She looks at Ritter in sheer disbelief.

"I keep telling you, Cin," Ritter says, "Magic is never free. Everybody pony up and pay the man."

TONIGHT'S SPECIAL

Lena follows Luciana Monrovio through the corridors of Gluttony Bay. Along the wall to her left, EMPLOYEES ONLY is painted in six-foot-tall red letters. To her right, floor-to-ceiling picture windows look out onto the black water of the bay in the evening.

"Where are you taking me?" she asks the neon-green succubus.

"It's time to go to work!" Monrovio informs her brightly.

"What the hell does that mean?"

Her tone remains sterile and pleasant, but there's a crack of impatience somewhere in it. "You'll find out soon enough."

Lena stops. "I'm not walking another step until you tell me what the fuck is happening."

Monrovio's hand is around her throat before Lena even registers movement. Her fingers are like knives and her grip is a steel collar. She lifts Lena a foot off the ground with that single hand, holding her there easily. Lena bats futilely at Monrovio's arm, gripping the sleeve of her suit to pry it loose, but it's useless.

"You listen to me, you little bitch," Luciana hisses at her as she squeezes the breath from Lena's neck. "You and your band of misfits have embarrassed me for the last time. And I do mean the *last* time. You don't want to walk? Fine. I'll break both of your fucking legs and drag you by that dehydrated rat's nest you call hair. Do you understand me?"

Lena can't form words, but she tries to nod.

"Very good, then," Luciana says pleasantly.

Monrovio releases her. Lena drops to her knees, clutching her throat and gasping for air.

"Take as long as you need, my dear," Luciana offers, her voice returning to that empty cordiality.

Lena stands, slowly, her eyes burning as they stare up at the monster in boardroom chic standing in front of her.

Monrovio clasps both hands around the handle of her attaché case, holding it in front of her and waiting.

Fists balled and knuckles white, Lena turns and begins walking, slowly.

Satisfied, Luciana treks on, leading her past the picturesque expanse of the bay. They walk down a windowless incline that ends in a pair of industrial clean-room doors. Lena watches as Monrovio enters a code on a touchscreen pad and scans her thumbprint. Air hisses and the doors part from the center, sliding into the walls.

Monrovio graciously motions Lena through.

She immediately feels an intense cold, not like a freezer but enough to raise goose bumps on her flesh. The space beyond is dark save for circular fluorescent lights that seem to illuminate only small areas, like spotlights. Something clinks beneath Lena's foot and she halts, looking down to see a large drain. The white-tiled floor is pockmarked with them.

She looks up. Dozens of oversized stainless steel bathtubs are bolted to the floor at regular intervals. Thick links of chrome chain ending in restraints sway idly above each tub. Not twenty yards from her stands a massive rack of cutting and bludgeoning implements: knives, cleavers, cudgels, and even cattle prods. The instruments are so clean and polished, they shine even in the darkened space.

"Welcome, Miss Tarr! I'm glad to see the trip agreed with you!"

Allensworth is waiting for them with Bronko.

Lena rushes forward.

"Chef!" she calls to him, grateful relief in her voice.

It's short-lived.

The pair is standing in front of the only tub whose chains aren't unburdened. A long bundle dangles, suspended in the air, wrapped from end to end in thick black cloth.

Lena's brain doesn't want to acknowledge that it can only be a person concealed under there.

Bronko takes gentle hold of her chin and turns her head from side to side, examining her face. He scowls at her swollen cheek and cut lip, at the fresh bruises on her neck left by Monrovio's fingers.

"What did they do?" he asks.

Lena pulls her chin away from his hand, shaking her head. "I'm fine."

"Miss Tarr is full of surprises," Allensworth interjects. "But then, we've learned that time and time again since she was taken under your wing, Byron."

"Where are we, Chef?" Lena asks Bronko. "What the hell is Gluttony Bay?"

Bronko stares darkly at Allensworth as he answers. "It's a restaurant . . . one that serves people."

"The finest human fare in the western hemisphere," Allensworth confirms without hesitation or shame. "And one of the most ultra-exclusive dining experiences in the world, reserved for only our closest friends and most important allies."

Bronko looks at him in abject disgust. "This is where folks taken to that CIA black site across the bay end up, ain't it? Accusin' folks of being terrorists and enemies of the state so you can serve 'em as dinner to things even worse 'n that."

Allensworth's smile only widens. "First of all, it's a military prison. Secondly, why do you think the prison has never been closed down, despite the public outcry?"

"Jesus." Lena's mind is reeling. "Oh my god, those . . . those people back there that I saw . . . the ones stuffing themselves . . ."

"They're a delicacy of the house," Monrovio explains. "Gluttony Bay is world-renowned for their sugar-fed Mediterranean beef."

Lena feels her stomach performing backflips and she has to press a hand against it to stem the wave of nausea.

"This is sick," Bronko says.

"By whose standards, Byron?" Bronko asks. "A cow would be appalled by the mere concept of a steakhouse, after all."

"People ain't cows."

"That depends on whom you ask. The food chain in our world is not so simple as that in the mundane world. It's my job to accommodate all species . . . of appetite."

Lena steps in front of Bronko. "So, what, we're on the menu, Allensworth? Is that it?"

He actually throws his head back and laughs. "My dear, no! You're the chefs, not dinner!"

"Then what do you expect is gonna happen here?" Bronko asks.

"We're going to clarify a few things that desperately

need clarifying. The first is the misapprehension you've apparently been laboring under that you have the ability to hide things from me. You do not. I know *everything*. I have known everything. I know you substituted a fast food recipe for the angel you were ordered to serve at the banquet for the Vig'nerash and Oexial clans. I know that doddering old hybrid woman you keep around as some kind of Sunday school teacher spiked the food for the royal goblin wedding. I know you've had our new Sceadu president's ear."

"Yeah, well, we know a few things too," Lena fires back. "Like you tried to use us to poison Consoné's followers, and when that didn't work, you brainwashed Darren into trying to kill Consoné himself."

"That's what I *do*, my dear," Allensworth impatiently corrects her. "That's what you're *for*. You serve whatever means I deem fit. In return, you are paid exorbitantly to practice the craft you love on a level unseen by most humans throughout history, and you are allowed access to tiers of society a little person like yourself would otherwise never even know existed. That you don't understand nor appreciate that exchange only demonstrates a fundamental entitlement on your part."

"I feed people; I don't kill 'em," Bronko insists.

Allensworth raises an eyebrow. "Do you really want to discuss the blood on your hands, Byron?"

Lena looks up at him, but Bronko doesn't answer.

"It's a base lack of appreciation," Allensworth continues. "That's simply what it comes down to. You two have no appreciation for what you've been given, what you have, or the lengths to which I go to facilitate and protect your simple little lives. Byron, you used to. But it seems ever since you hired this young woman, she's infected you with—"

"Morals?" Lena offers, sarcastically.

"My dear," Allensworth says, "this evening, I intend to demonstrate that your compass in that arena is sorely lacking true north. You can't judge a thing until you truly know its scale. And you've been paddling around in the kiddy pool of moral decisions."

Allensworth reaches up and grabs a handful of the garb wrapped around the figure suspended above the tub. With one powerful jerk, he tears away the black shroud, casting it aside.

"Darren!" Lena screams, immediately rushing forward, only to be restrained by Bronko.

"Hold on now, girl!" he warns her.

Darren hangs upside-down, naked, with his wrists bound behind his back. His head and face have both been shaved smooth, and he wears an undersized muzzle compressing his mouth and jaw and rendering him unable to speak. Not that it matters, as he's currently unconscious.

"What is this?" Bronko demands, still holding Lena at bay.

"Tonight's special!" Monrovio happily informs them. "And you'll be preparing it!"

"You motherfucker!" Lena spits at Allensworth.

He's unmoved. "This evening, the two of you are going to learn just how lucky you are in your current cushy little stations. You're going to learn how genuinely *unburdened* you are and how truly insignificant your petty little moral dilemmas become in the grand scheme. You're going to understand the realities of our world, the real world, and you're going to experience a taste . . . pardon the pun . . . of just how flexible those vaunted morals of yours can be."

Bronko looks from Darren's helpless face to Allensworth. "You really think I'll kill this boy for you?"

"No, Byron, I think Miss Tarr will, and you'll help her prepare him for tonight's guests at Gluttony Bay. Mexican will be a rare treat for them."

Lena stares at him in shock and then looks frantically up at Bronko.

"Stop this now," he tells Allensworth.

"It will *stop*," Allensworth insists, "when Miss Tarr proves beyond a shadow of a doubt she can fall in line, take orders, and do what needs to be done. If she cannot, then she can no longer serve our needs. If she cannot, she will also be put on the menu tonight, and you'll cook alone, Byron. And if *you* can't bring yourself to do it, then I will rain fire down upon that decrepit pile of bricks you call a company and everyone inside it. I will raze every single member of your staff to ash and contract a company on which I can depend."

"You're out of your fucking mind," Lena says.

Allensworth sighs. "Look where you are, my dear. Sanity is a relative concept. Your problem is you're attempting to apply the purely human world's logic to a world where humans are ants. To rise above, the ants must adapt."

He gives a pointed nod to Luciana.

"Now, Miss Tarr, I know you're a talented young chef, but have you ever butchered before? And I mean farm-to-table here."

Monrovio goes to the tool rack and places her attaché case on the tiled floor. She selects a large, razor-edged butcher's knife and holds it aloft between two hands. Rejoining them, she presents the instrument to Lena.

"You'll first need to drain Mister Vargas," Allensworth continues. "One quick, forceful swipe of the blade across his throat will do the trick. We've done the tedious prep work for you, as you can see."

Lena stares down at the knife being offered to her by the succubus, her breath coming in staccato bursts.

"It's time to decide, Lena," Allensworth tells her in

a more serious tone. "Either you're part of the team or you're not. If you're not, then as Miss Monrovio said, you're on the menu."

"Damn you for this, you bastard," Bronko curses him, helplessly.

"Being damned has its privileges, Byron," Allensworth says, echoing Bronko's own words. "You of all people know that."

Lena turns her head and looks up at Bronko, lost. There are tears welling in the corners of her eyes.

"Chef?"

Bronko swallows, hard. He looks down on her with all the love and pain and sympathy in the world.

"I know you love him," he whispers to her. "But he's already dead, Lena. You have to think of it like that. You didn't do this. You didn't do any of it. It's not your fault, no matter what. But Darren is dead either way. I don't want it to be both of you, and it doesn't have to be."

She blinks at him in disbelief, unable to process or accept that it's him saying these words to her.

"Chef . . . I can't . . ."

"You remember what Consoné said. It's war. You've been there. You know what it takes to survive."

"Not this," Lena pleads with him.

There are tears in Bronko's eyes now. "I can't fix this. I'm sorry."

Lena knows it's true. For months, she's dreaded the moment when Bronko's stroke would run out and they'd face a lethal situation beyond anyone's control.

Now it's come, and it's far worse than any of her nightmares.

"It's time, Miss Tarr," Allensworth says. "We have hungry diners waiting."

Lena turns from Bronko, staring down once again at the gleaming blade of the knife held in Luciana Monrovio's hands. She looks past the succubus at Darren, seeing ten years of her life and their friendship in his tormented face.

Lena reaches out and closes her hand around the handle of the knife. She feels Bronko's hand squeezing her shoulder, trying in vain to comfort her.

"I'm sorry, Darren," she rasps through the tears.

She wants to believe he can hear her, but Lena knows in that moment, she'll never speak with her friend again.

PART III

MAN DOWN

FLOCK OF SEAGULLS

The helicopter's pilot is a pudgy, aviator-shades-clad gremlin chewing on an amber-lit stogie and sitting on three phone books. Ritter introduced him to the team as "Ruby" upon takeoff, and although they seemed dubious, no one could argue with the government-issued wings clipped to his tiny (and, according to Cindy, "adorable") bomber jacket and the front of his equally tiny (and again, adorable) pilot's cap.

They're somewhere over the Florida Keys. The cutting of the chopper's blades is deafening, and the air whipping through the open cabin of the military surplus vehicle beats against their exposed flesh. Ritter has instructed Ruby to double-time it the whole way, and the gremlin war vet isn't letting him down.

The brothers Thane have donned their fatigues for the first time since slogging through jungles of South America together fighting rogue brujos and brujas employed by the drug cartels. Though Ritter's team has never carried firearms (owing largely to their wide margin of inefficacy in repelling supernatural creatures and mystical forces), Marcus is toting Ritter's pump-action shotgun loaded with dragon bone–filled rounds.

Marcus leans close to shout in Ritter's ear over the blade song. "Just so we're clear, and not that I'm complaining or anything, but your plan is to fly this slick right up to a heavily fortified military prison that's also a pipeline for a cannibal restaurant for the super-mega-extra-human-elite and just . . . land?"

"Basically," Ritter shouts back, managing to sound indifferent even while yelling at the top of his lungs.

Marcus just stares at him in silence for several long moments.

Then: "You're fucking with me, right?"

Ritter shakes his head.

Marcus holds up two thumbs in mock enthusiasm. "Awesome!"

Next to Ritter, Cindy is passing the time by sharpening the blade of her tactical tomahawk with a cylindrical whetstone. It's one of several blades sheathed in scabbards configured to her flak jacket and webbed belt. They're mostly combat knives, although several throwing weapons coated in black ceramic are concealed within reach from any of several positions in which she might find herself once they're inside.

There's also a rucksack filled with a cereal variety pack

of explosives resting between her feet.

Hara, who takes up three seats and is the reason Ruby had to trim two hundred pounds of weight off his bird before takeoff, is examining a hand-drawn layout of Gluttony Bay under the glow of a soft blue ChemLight. It's in Ritter's hand, composed from several secondhand sources, several of them people and creatures who'd only heard details of the place from others who had supposedly seen the inside of it.

Ever the minimalist, Hara is clad in a simple BDU sweater, black jeans, and moccasins. The only weapons he carries are his hands.

Moon is, at Cindy's request, heavily strapped into his seat. His fledging "alchemist's kit" is slung around his neck, and although none of them have seen its contents, Moon assures them it's essential equipment for a mission like this. Of course, he'd probably also say the same thing about the bag of Cool Ranch Doritos from which he's currently chomping five chips at a time.

"Seriously, man, what're we doing?" Marcus presses.

"My intel says the restaurant is an entirely separate structure from the prison, so as long as we're in and out, we shouldn't incur any military resistance. I glamoured the chopper before we took off," Ritter explains. "We won't show up on radar, and anyone spotting us from the air won't see a helicopter."

"What'll they see? We're not invisible, are we?"

Ritter shakes his head. "We're a flock of seagulls."

The implication hits Marcus, and he breathes a huge sigh of relief.

"Nice, bro! Fuckin' hated that band, but nice!"

Ritter just nods.

Marcus hesitates, but he can't shake the remaining thought from his mind.

"Hey, Ritt!"

His brother just stares back at him, blank-faced and waiting.

"I'm sorry for my part in all this shit. I didn't mean to fuck up your situation."

Ritter is already shaking his head before Marcus finishes. "What's happening would've happened with or without you. The only difference is Lena wouldn't be pissed at me. I won't pretend I don't wish that part hadn't happened."

"Well, I'm sorry about that part, then."

Ritter nods. "I know. Look, we've both made a lot of the same mistakes. I'm just older and I got to make a bunch of them before you. Let's call it even, all right?"

Marcus looks genuinely relieved. "Thanks, man."

"No worries."

A moment later: "Hey, Ritt?"

"Yeah?"

"Is Cindy single, or . . ." Marcus asks.

The look Ritter flashes him could wilt houseplants.

"Too soon," Marcus admits. "I get it."

EXECUTIONER'S CHOICE

"I recommend taking firm hold of the back of Mr. Vargas's head with one hand while slicing with the other," Allensworth offers helpfully.

Lena hefts the two-foot butcher's knife she's accepted from Luciana Monrovio. The weight is tremendous, but the balance is perfect. Its edge is razor thin and catches even the errant light from the overhead fluorescent spots.

"I'm sorry, Darren," she says, staring past Monrovio at her best friend's unconscious, upside-down face.

She means it, too. She's sorry she's let it come to this, for both of them.

She can feel Bronko's hand, large and rough from their everyday work, like her father's. He squeezes her shoulder reassuringly.

Lena nods, accepting his comfort and counsel, accepting the situation and what she has to do.

She reaches up and seizes Monrovio by the back of the succubus' neck with her empty hand, drawing the woman forward and thrusting up with the butcher's knife. The razor-sharp instrument's impossibly long blade pierces Monrovio beneath her chin, puncturing her soft palate and skewering her tongue. It enters the roof of her mouth easily and half a second later glides smoothly and devastatingly into her brain.

"Stop!" Allensworth yells in genuine alarm.

He sounds very far away to Lena in that moment, but a part of her relishes in the shock she's inspired.

Lena grits her teeth as she rips the knife free of Luciana's skull with great effort. The neon green of her suit jacket is overtaken by blood as black as an eclipsed sun. She drops to her knees, swaying there like a top that's done spinning. Monrovio's eyes are wide open, but they focus on nothing, glazed and empty. In the next moment, they've filled with the same black blood.

Lena turns the stained knife on Allensworth menacingly. She has no intention of making the same mistake she did back at her and Darren's apartment. She didn't take her shot then, and it cost them all.

Unfortunately, before she can advance on him, her attention is drawn behind them. Without warning, several figures emerge from the shadows of the kill floor, more of those plastic-faced attendants in their shock trooper smocks. They're unarmed but move with predatory grace and intention.

Bronko intercepts the first one, picking him up and slamming him to the floor like a professional wrestler.

The impact is such that the tile beneath the attendant's body cracks in places, shatters in others. Bronko quickly raises a booted foot and stomps several times on the man's head and face, caving in the mannequin features of his mask.

Meanwhile, an attendant twice her size advances on Lena. He seems totally unprepared when, without the slightest hesitation, she shoves the entire length of her blade into his chest. The attendant collapses forward, and Lena has to sidestep to avoid being felled under him. She can't pull her knife free in time, however, and its handle is forced from her hand.

The third attendant wraps his arms around her from behind and lifts Lena into the air. She struggles, kicking at his legs with her heels, but before she can even formulate a plan, his arms disappear from her body and she lands back on her feet. Whipping around, she watches as Bronko, holding the masked man by the throat and head, gruesomely and with sheer force breaks his neck.

The sound of bone ripping from bone causes her to cringe. Lena is left staring at Bronko like a child. Making her peace with killing has been a horrific enough internal process for her, but watching him, a mentor and even father figure, commit the same brutality unsettles Lena in an entirely new way.

There's no time to dwell on it. The corner of her eye

catches movement, and Lena turns to see Allensworth attempting to casually stroll from the room. She quickly kneels down and pulls the blade free of the attendant's chest, leaping over his body and running up behind the fleeing rat that masterminded all of this.

Lena grabs Allensworth by the back of his collar with a bloody hand and halts him, pressing the tip of the blade into the small of his back.

"Tell me again how to butcher a human being," she bids him in a shaking, rage-filled voice. "Tell me now."

"Tarr, don't kill him," Bronko orders her. "We need him."

"More than you shall ever know," Allensworth says, ever weary, only to have Lena painfully jab him in the back.

"Yes, Chef," Lena says. "For now."

As she holds him at bay, Bronko has already moved over to where Darren is still suspended in the air. He carefully climbs up onto the embalmer's tub, balancing his large booted feet on opposite edges as he reaches up to unlatch Darren's ankles from where they're hung on a hook.

"How do we get out of here?" Lena asks Allensworth.

"You don't, Miss Tarr, with or without me. This is one of the most secure facilities on the planet. Unless you're a VIP guest dining in the restaurant, there is no exit from this bay."

"Then how do the guests come and go?"

"By private helicopter."

"Okay. You'll take us to the landing pad."

"That won't help. If you try to commandeer an incoming or outgoing helicopter, you'll certainly be killed."

"Then it'll be on my terms, not yours."

"You're rationalizing, Miss Tarr."

"No, I'm holding a big fucking knife against your spine, so shut your mouth."

She punctuates the statement with a pricking jab that causes Allensworth to jump.

Bronko has hauled Darren down and quickly swaddled him in the same black cloth with which Allensworth's people mummified him. He slings Darren's body over one broad shoulder like a firearm and turns to Lena and Allensworth.

"Let's go," he says simply.

"Byron," Allensworth ventures tentatively, "you have to have more sense than this young woman—"

"Like she said," he interrupts the man, "if we die here, it's on our terms. Now, if I were you, I'd walk before this 'young lady' makes her some kidney pies."

Lena grins up at him, despite everything.

"Yes, Chef," she says, and prods their hostage forward.

WALK-INS

The sentry's mask splits in half as Cindy swings the blade of her tomahawk into his face, the impact alone folding his padded knees and knocking him down to the rooftop.

Cindy places a booted foot against the sentry's flak jacketed chest and uses it for leverage to yank her axe blade free.

"Ain't that a bitch?" she asks his still form. "One minute you're admiring a flock of seagulls, the next an angry black woman with an axe leaps out at you and that's your whole ass right there. Shit!"

Cindy quickly ducks as the body of another sentry goes flying a sparse inch above her head. It collides with the top of a ventilation shaft, and what's left of the man falls to the roof, limbs twisted like a rag doll.

She looks over at Hara, who booked the sentry's abrupt flight.

"Really, man?" she asks.

Hara shrugs by way of an apology.

Ritter and Marcus are already pulling bundles of nylon rope and climbing rigs out of rucksacks.

"Cindy!" Ritter calls to her across the rooftop. "Work fast! We're over the side in sixty seconds!"

Cindy nods, unzipping a black bag slung around from her shoulder and removing an octagonal charge the size of her palm. She quickly slaps it between her booted feet, a magnetic plate on its backside adhering the charge to the metallic insulation beneath the rooftop's surface. She dashes thirty yards ahead, laying another charge there. Fifty-seven seconds later, she has sprinted from corner to corner and blanketed the entire rooftop at strategic structural points with a dozen identical devices.

"Everybody hook up!" Ritter orders them.

"I'm thinkin' I'll wait with the chopper," Moon says. "Y'know, in case the gremlin gets lonely."

"Seeing as how Moon on the end of a rappelling rig basically becomes a yo-yo, I'm inclined to let the boy slide on this one," Cindy tells Ritter.

"Fine," he says. "If Ruby has any trouble up here, hit us on the radio."

"I can totally do that," Moon assures him.

"What is he for, again?" Marcus asks as they all slip into their repelling gear.

"He eats weird shit," Cindy explains.

Marcus nods. "That actually makes a weird kind of sense, considering what y'all do."

"Does it?" Cindy asks.

"Thanks, Cin," Moon says, sulkily.

"Anytime, boo."

———————

"Dinner is served!" Alfonse grandly announces to the long table occupied by stylish demon warriors.

Behind the hooded host, servers wheel out massive human rib cages hoisted upright on two vertical spits apiece. The meat between their bones is crackling brown and still steaming.

There are animalistic sounds of approval from the Vig'nerash clan members.

One of the servers, barbeque fork and carving knife in hand, leans over the rib cage. He pauses just short of piercing the cooked flesh, staring through the slits in his face mask and out of the panoramic window composing the entire bay wall of the restaurant.

Cindy, tethered by a thin line of nylon cord, seems to glide on the air itself toward the outside of the window. She lands against the reinforced panes with the soles of her boots. The noise on the inside barely registers. The nearest patrons, in fact, don't even look up from their meals.

"Uh ... Señor Alfonse," the server tries to warn the host, who is occupied with schmoozing the Vig'nerash elder at the head of the table.

Cindy slaps something against the outside of the window, and whatever it is sticks there, a small red light flashing on it. She bends her knees and kicks away from the glass, hard, putting as much distance between it and herself as possible.

"Señor Alfonse!" the server exclaims.

"What is it, Marco?" Alfonse demands impatiently.

In answer, Marco points at the bay.

Alfonse looks up just as the entire middle section of the restaurant's towering picture window cracks and then shatters altogether, glass shards hailing through the dining room and covering the tables, patrons, and staff.

There's shrieking from the ghouls and confused, angry outbursts from the humans. When Cindy swings back through the window, the rest of the team is on their own ropes right beside her. Once they're all inside, they detach themselves from the ropes and drop to the floor of the restaurant, Hara taking two tables with him as he does.

"Everybody down!" Ritter thunders at the patrons and staff. "Everybody hit the floor now! Now, now, now!"

Marcus racks his shotgun to punctuate his brother's command, firing a warning shot into the ceiling that causes emeralds to rain down over them all.

The humans and ghouls are quick to cower beneath

their tables or in their booths, but the Vig'nerash demons hesitate. Several are hovering inches above their seats, growls rumbling in their scaly throats.

Marcus levels the muzzle of his shotgun at the nearest demon warrior and racks the weapon's heavy slide.

"Who wants to play 'How Bad Can I Fuck Up a Demon's Eurotrash Suit?'" Marcus asks him.

The warriors all sit back down.

"Let's go!" Ritter says to the rest of his team.

They quickly and cleanly sweep through the dining room, and Ritter hits the doors to the kitchen first, kicking them apart. He and Marcus hold them open for the others, Marcus covering their flanks with his shotgun.

By the time he joins the rest of the team inside, the kitchen doors swinging closed behind Marcus, Ritter and the others have stopped moving. They're bunched together just inside the doors, and Marcus nearly plows right into their collected backs as he breaks into a sprint, still laboring under the notion they're sweeping through the facility with all haste.

"What the hell, guys?" he hisses at them.

Cindy's and Ritter's shoulders part in front of him, and Marcus finds himself taking in the same sight as the rest of them, and like the rest of them, it stops Marcus cold.

There is no blood. There are no screams. Stark white hazardous materials suits and particle-filtering masks wholly obscure the "chefs" working in the Gluttony Bay kitchen. They go about their grisly tasks in calm and efficient silence. The far wall is lined with a wide-stretching row of tall, clear cylindrical chambers. They're filled with superheated water boiling uncovered. Steadily deteriorating human bodies occupy each one. Those bodies have been shaved of all body hair and surgically cleaned like wild game, the flaps made of their torsos wafting over hollowed cavities beneath. The layers of their flesh have loosened and separated. Shiny aluminum staircases lead up to a catwalk that skims across the tops of the cylinders. The human fare is fished out in pieces by the hazmat workers, who pull the bodies apart with long, razor-sharp pole instruments, and delivered to stainless steel cooking stations for preparation.

It is somehow far worse than the fairy-tale horror-show cannibalism of people chained to butcher's blocks and gargantuan black steel cauldrons bubbling with human soup. This is clinical and sanitized and completely detached. It is thoroughly inhuman horror, the kind manufactured in concentration camps where sadism is transformed into purposeful and industrial genocide, and where even the base humanity of being a victim is taken away as people are reduced to cattle.

"Motherfuckers," Marcus curses, racking the shotgun's slide and putting the butt to his shoulder tightly, his finger tensing against the weapon's trigger.

The first swarm of buckshot he unleashes shatters the center cylinder and floods the kitchen with scalding water and what has mostly been reduced to a skeleton. The cooks in their hazmat suits flee from its path, although several of them feel the stinging droplets splattered against their few exposed patches of skin. Marcus once again racks the slide and blasts the cylinders at either end of the row, the sudden boiling tidal waves forcing the sterile butchers into the center of the kitchen, where they begin falling over one another like lobsters in a tank. Marcus continues expelling empty shells and pumping fresh ones into the shotgun's chamber, emptying it of ammo as he destroys every last human pot in the kitchen, bathing the now-shrieking cooks in lavalike water.

Ritter looks beyond the chaos, spotting another set of doors set into the far corner of the kitchen.

"Let's move!" he orders them all. "We can't do any more here. We have to find our people."

Marcus looks at his brother, the younger sibling's ordinarily dark eyes appearing absolutely black in that moment. He nods silently, retrieving new shells from the ammo bag affixed to his belt and reloading the shotgun on the move.

Ritter and Hara follow, but Cindy lingers behind a moment longer. She pulls her bag in front of her body by its shoulder strap, unzips and upends it, spilling several octagonal charges onto the kitchen floor. Zipping the sack closed and shoving it behind her back, she spares one final, disgusted look at the half-drowned cannibal cooks wallowing in scorching pain among the gutted and flesh-stripped skeletal remains of their victims.

"Better than y'all deserve," she mutters to herself through gritted teeth.

Her boots splash across the wet floor as she hustles to catch up with the rest of her team.

DOUBLE-BOOKED

The elevator careens between the upper floors of Gluttony Bay with the force of a slow train. Its attendant is curled up in one corner; Bronko didn't kill him, but he did hit him hard enough to cause the man's brain to smack against the inside of his skull.

"I'm curious," Allensworth says, his voice tighter and more cautious than they're used to hearing it, probably because Lena's still holding a knife to his back. "Let us suppose you succeed in extricating yourself from Gluttony Bay. Let us even suppose you return to the warm confines of your beloved Sin du Jour safely. Then what? And what happens to me? Do you intend to kill me in cold blood, Byron?"

"You killed me in cold blood," Bronko reminds him.

"That was different. I knew you'd come back."

"It damn sure didn't feel different."

Lena has no idea what they're talking about, but she also knows this is no time to inquire.

"Very well," Allensworth relents. "You kill me in cold blood. Then what? What do you imagine happens next?"

"Maybe I'll start a food truck," Bronko muses. "Somewhere in the Southwest, say."

"Byron," Allensworth chastises.

Bronko ignores him. "I could use a sous chef on the truck, Tarr."

Lena smiles weakly. "Sounds good to me, Chef."

The elevator stops, its touchscreen display indicating they've reached the top level, the helipad.

Lena tenses as the doors in front of them part, preparing to rush Allensworth by the collar out onto the platform at high speed.

She doesn't even take her first step toward the doors.

"Jam it up my ass sideways," Bronko whispers to himself in pure dread.

There must be thirty of them, all draped in executioner's hoods and all of them as large as Bronko or bigger. They wear leather gloves up to their elbows and all carry oversized meat cleavers and machete-sized knives. They're gathered shoulder to shoulder just five feet outside the elevator doors, so thick neither Bronko nor Lena can see the helipad beyond.

"I tried to warn you," Allensworth says. "What would you like to do now, Byron?"

Bronko gently shifts Darren's weight over his shoulder, carrying the younger man obviously beginning to wear him down. He doesn't answer Allensworth's question.

"Miss Tarr, then?" Allensworth calls behind him. "What's it to be, Lena? Shall we go back downstairs and try this again, my way? I'm willing to excuse your dispatching Miss Monrovio. She was an outside hire, anyway. We can still salvage our relationship *and* your careers. I give you my word."

Lena looks up at Bronko, trying to stuff down the panic she's feeling, determined to act from here forward with resolve.

Bronko's eyes are hard and soft at the same time, soft for Lena and all that's happened, and hard for what has to happen now.

He nods.

She nods back.

"Miss Tarr, my leniency will only extend so long before—"

"I gave my word, too," Lena says.

She runs him through, piercing his back with her large butcher's blade and skewering his kidney.

Allensworth tenses and groans, arching against her helplessly as she perforates him. Outside the elevator, the brutes roar with rage and lethal intention. Lena raises her left leg and places a boot against Allensworth's ass, ripping her blade free and kicking him through the doors at the same time. He collides with the nearest brutes rushing the car, knocking them off balance and bottlenecking the rest for just a moment.

It's long enough for Lena to press the right button on the touchscreen. The doors close with half a dozen hooded faces inches from it, and the elevator begins to descend.

"What now, Chef?" Lena asks.

Bronko crouches down and, gently as possible, sets Darren's still unconscious form in the corner of the car, breathing easier now that he's unburdened. He stands with a groan, stretching out his spine and pressing both hands into his back.

"I don't know, Tarr. I just don't know. I guess we see where the doors open and go from there."

"Is he dead, at least? Did I kill him?"

"Allensworth? If he can die, he's dead, yeah."

"You'd think I'd learn not to take anything for granted by now," Lena says, attempting a joke, but neither of them has a laugh left in them.

The elevator *ding*s gently, almost delicately. It seems an absurdly benign sound under the circumstances. Both Bronko and Lena tense at the ready for whatever comes, Lena pressing both hands tightly around the handle of her large knife in preparation to swing it like a sword at the first brute through the doors.

When they finally part and she sees the faces waiting for them on the other side, Lena instead winds up dropping her knife altogether. It hits the elevator floor length-wise, clattering loudly.

"Ritter?" Bronko says in utter disbelief.

Marcus lowers his shotgun as the rest of the team stares into the car in an equal amount of surprise.

Lena rushes forward, almost throwing herself at Ritter. She clings to him, all forgotten, and presses her face into his neck. She cries there, openly, ignoring the eyes on them when she normally would be horrified by so many people, especially those she knows, seeing her break down in such a way.

Ritter doesn't protest. He holds her against him grate-fully, letting her exorcise the last few days in the only way she can.

"It's real good to see y'all," Bronko tells the rest of them.

"It's good to see you too, boss," Cindy says. "We need to move."

"Back the way you came?"

She shakes her head. "Too many hostiles."

"Then how're we getting out?"

"We've got a glamoured chopper," Ritter informs him, still holding Lena. "We'll blow out another set of those bay-facing windows and I'll call it down."

Bronko nods thoughtfully. "I can accommodate ya on that score. Climb on in."

GO

In clear defiance of the EMPLOYEES ONLY painted on the wall, Bronko, Lena, and Ritter's team rushes into the same corridor through which Luciana Monrovio escorted Lena what seems like an eternity ago to her now. Hara has placed Darren's still unconscious form easily over one of the giant's extra-wide shoulders. Ritter tucks a two-way communicator back inside his fatigues after summoning Ruby from the rooftop.

Cindy runs ahead, to what she judges to be the center point of the corridor. She unzips her black bag and begins setting a large expanse of the picture window pane with charges.

The rest of them catch up with her just as she's finished securing the last one. Outside the windows, a dense flock of seagulls descends into view. They all hover there unnaturally, flapping their wings but not going anywhere, simply waiting several yards from the outside of the glass.

"That's our ride!" Ritter informs them all. "Cindy, blow it!"

"Shit," they hear Marcus utter.

Everyone stops, looking up and down the corridor.

At both ends, deep swells of hooded brutes brandishing their large butchering blades have appeared. There must be at least sixty men and women between them, and they've completely cut off both ends of the corridor.

Both sides begin to advance.

"Everybody down!" Cindy yells.

Bronko, Lena, and the rest of the team drop to the floor as she detonates her charges. The glass explodes, blasting them with shards and the sudden harsh winds from the bay. The sudden impact momentarily halts the brute squads, even causing them to backpedal for a moment.

Marcus raises his shotgun and levels its muzzle at the group up the hall.

"I'll cover!" he yells to Ritter.

A powerful hand completely encompasses the barrel and feeding tube of the shotgun, lowering it with ease.

Hara looks down at Marcus and shakes his head.

"Go," he says to Ritter and the others.

Marcus looks to his brother, confused, and Ritter stares back at Hara.

"Are you sure?" he asks the giant.

"Go!"

Even at full volume, Hara's voice is surprisingly quiet for a creature of his immense power and size.

They watch as Hara passes off Darren's body to

Bronko. He then strips off his sweater and the tank top beneath. His expansive torso is covered in tattoos: not ink, but deliberate scars raised to form concentric circular patterns in his flesh, like a sea of mazes that all lead to one center point.

Hara turns to face the nearest group of brutes. If the blast gave them pause, the sight of him stripped to the waist and ready for battle actually has them reconsidering. It lasts only a moment, regardless, and then the first wave begins surging forward again.

With a deep, guttural cry of war, Hara balls up his fist and springs forward with shocking speed, rushing them headlong. He collides with the first three, knocking them over with the ease of bowling pins.

Outside, the seagulls edge ever closer to the open section of window.

"Everybody go!" Ritter orders the others.

Marcus is the first to leap through, disappearing into the flock. Cindy follows him with a nod to Ritter. Lena hesitates, not wanting to leave Bronko and Darren, but Ritter takes her by the arm and practically tosses her out through the window.

"Can you make it with him?" he asks Bronko.

"Let's find out," Bronko says, clasping both arms around Darren's body and leaping out of the window.

They both disappear into the glamour of birds.

The second brigade of brutes has reached their exit point, and Ritter turns just in time to duck an incoming swipe of a meat cleaver. He launches a kick into the face of the hood that swung it, knocking him back into two other brutes.

Ritter turns back to the blasted windows. His eye catches one final glimpse of Hara mowing down hoods and taking blades to his broad and scarred back before Ritter is forced to leap away from the mob behind him, sailing out the window and landing inside the cabin of the chopper.

"Welcome back, ladies and gentlemen!" Moon greets them happily. "Hey, where's Hara?"

"Are we all aboard?" Ruby calls to Ritter from the cockpit in his frog-throated gremlin's voice.

Cindy looks at Ritter desperately, her eyes insisting they can't leave Hara behind.

He's staring right back into her eyes, his own as hard as stone, when he answers their pilot.

"We're full up! Take her out of here!"

Ruby nods, pulling back on the stick and climbing the chopper into the air.

Twenty feet up, the helicopter suddenly stalls with a violent jerk. More than that, it feels as though they've been pulled down.

"What the fuck?" Marcus swears.

"Ruby, what's happening?" Ritter calls to the gremlin. "Are we hung up? Did they hook us?"

"I don't know! I've got no warnin' lights!"

Ruby wrestles with the controls, and a moment later, they're climbing smoothly again.

"I guess not," Ritter says.

They all fall silent, which is how they're all able to hear it when Hara's hand appears above the edge of the open cabin and slams down on the floor.

No one can believe it as he pulls his giant, dripping-red frame inside the cabin. Ritter and Marcus and Cindy all rush to help drag him the rest of the way aboard. He's slashed and punctured in dozens of places, almost every inch of his body covered and his remaining clothing soaked in blood, most of it his.

"Jesus Harold fucking Christ," Marcus rants, "he jumped all the way onto the landing skids like this? That's fucking inhuman."

"Well, he is, and he's bleeding out!" Ritter yells at his brother.

"What do we do?" Cindy asks Ritter, helplessly. "I can't . . . Where do we even start?"

"Moon!" Ritter calls across the cabin. "Get that alchemist's kit and get over here!"

Moon stares back at him from his seat with wide, vacant eyes.

"Move, boy!" Cindy barks at him. "Now, dammit!"

Moon nervously unbuckles himself and practically flops onto the cabin deck, crawling over to them, small bag slung around his head.

"What . . . what can I do, man?" he asks Ritter. "I'm not really—"

"This is one-oh-one transference shit," Ritter insists. "I've seen that Irish lush do it a million times. It's just a lot of cuts instead of one. You can use me. Take my life and give it to him."

"Ritt, no!" Cindy insists.

"Just do it, Moon!"

"Ritter, I . . ."

"Don't worry about me!" Ritter orders him. "Just do it! Now!"

Moon looks at him, at a complete loss.

It occurs to Ritter in that moment that Moon isn't burdened by concern for Ritter's well-being.

Ritter reaches up and tears the shoulder bag from around Moon's neck. He practically rips it open, raining candy bars and canned sodas across the cabin floor.

They're the sack's sole contents.

"You told us you've been studying with Ryland," Cindy says in disbelief.

"We mostly drank," Moon admits. "Smoked weed. He told me stories with . . . with alchemy *in* them—"

"You piece of shit!" Cindy curses him. "You useless, lying little turd!"

"He didn't teach you anything?" Ritter asks, evenly.

Moon shakes his head, staring down in shame.

"That's that, then," Ritter says without emotion. "Nothing to be done."

He leans over Hara, who is barely conscious. Ritter takes one of the giant's hands in both of his and holds it close to his chest.

Cindy watches him in disbelief. She opens her mouth to protest, but realizes there are no solutions to offer, only blame and reproach, and neither of those will help Hara now. Instead, she takes Hara's other hand in hers, following Ritter's lead.

No one else speaks. Bronko holds Lena while she cradles Darren's swaddled form. Marcus sits back, watching his brother and Cindy console their dying friend. Moon stays splayed on all fours, head hung low. His tears begin to fall upon the deck.

Hara never speaks another word. His eyes, the color of sand touched by rain, hold Ritter's until they close for the final time.

"Go," Ritter urges him quietly, his voice barely a whisper.

Hara does.

After he's gone, Ritter carefully places Hara's hand

against the valley of his still chest. He leans down and kisses the giant's forehead.

Cindy follows his lead, returning Hara's other hand to the fallen warrior's body and gently pressing her palm over his eyes.

Ritter's darkened gaze meets hers and he nods. Cindy turns away from Hara's body and reaches inside her right boot, removing a small detonator no bigger than a cigarette lighter. The device is crowned with a single blue button covered by a safety cap. Cindy flips the cap open and smashes the tip of her thumb against that blue button.

In the steadily fading distance, the top of Gluttony Bay erupts in flame. It engulfs the entire roof, causing it to collapse through the rest of the structure. At the same time, a fiery tornado belches forth from the building's center where the kitchen is located, further gutting the edifice from within. Gluttony Bay, its structure catastrophically weakened and its façade and many floors on fire, implodes with the fury of a dying neutron star, all four corners caving in spectacularly.

Gathered around Hara's body, they all watch with hollow satisfaction from inside the chopper as the house of inhuman horror burns and topples into the bay. The notorious prison facing the explosion remains intact, its cold concrete and brittle-seeming fences silent and still on the other side of the water. Its barbed wire and high walls appear even more ominous cast in the fiery shadow of the steadily disintegrating cannibal cabal its tortured inmates will no longer feed.

Ruby speeds them away over the calm blue waters, and in minutes, the fire is little more than an amber memory sinking beyond the horizon.

WILLING DONOR

The Vig'nerash elder's name is Sircus, but you won't find it mentioned in any human literature or texts, no matter how arcane.

In traditional demon culture, one of the largest determining factors in one's status is how loud their name rings out in human religious mythology and folklore (it matters little whether any of the human's stories are *true*, mind you, as long as they got the demon's name right). The farther back in human history a demon's name can be found recorded, whether in language or image, the more status one has.

This is a primary reason the Vig'nerash clan shirks "traditional" demon culture at every turn.

Elder is also a relative term among the Vig'nerash clan, one held over from old-school demon clan practices. The Vig'nerash prefer to follow the strongest, savviest warrior among their ranks, not the most decrepit fossil still drawing breath on the mortal plane.

Perhaps Sircus never led a demonic army against an angelic battalion, or made a name for himself in some shit-smelling Old World country stealing babies from their cribs, but he *did* rip the spine from the backs of three of the finest warriors from his clutch to become the leader of the Vig'nerash.

He could crush the mandible of any dust-filled Oexial clan elder with one hand.

(He tells himself that every morning.)

Allensworth is lying on an ergonomic, biofeedback-responsive medical bed in a state-of-the-art infirmary. He's awake, his color has returned to normal, and he's currently taking delicate little sips from a children's box of tropical fruit juice. The surgical gown he's wearing is emblazoned with the Gluttony Bay logo and is one hundred percent Egyptian cotton.

Sircus stands over him, a smug grin on his reptilian face. He dabs at the corner of his mouth with a bloodred pocket square that matches his silk tie. The accessories stand out starkly against the dark Hugo Boss suit tailored to the bulky scales of his frame.

"You look well," the demon remarks.

"Thank you," Allensworth replies. "And as you are quite obviously aware, I owe you exclusively for that fact."

"Technically, you owe Vrrgon here."

Allensworth looks to his right. Lying on the bed neighboring his is a young Vig'nerash demon warrior. He's unconscious and has been stripped of his finely tailored Italian suit. Two fresh surgical scars peek above the surface of the mattress, running along his left and right sides.

"Will he live?" Allensworth asks.

Sircus shrugs. "I doubt it, and even if he does, he'll be useless as a warrior."

"Did I really need both of his kidneys?"

"No, but I don't believe in taking chances."

"Then how did you get him to volunteer?"

Sircus scratches at the scale covering his temple with the thinly pointed tip of a talon.

"Well," he begins, tentatively, "'volunteer' is what you humans call a subjective concept among demons."

"Meaning you probably ripped his kidneys out yourself."

"Are you complaining, my friend?"

"Oh, not at all. In fact, I must admit, I feel fantastic."

"That's because he did more than save you; he has improved you. You're part Vig'nerash now, however small those parts may be. You'll find the benefits . . . to your liking. Mostly, anyway."

Allensworth raises an eyebrow. "Mostly?"

Sircus waves his clawed hand dismissively. "Don't worry about that now. The point is you're alive when you otherwise would not be, and you have promises to keep."

Allensworth's eyes darken. "You are correct. I do."

"I meant to *me*," Sircus says. "Revenge on those who did this to you does not concern me. It's a petty matter held against our business."

"I am aware of that," Allensworth assures him. "I'll settle the former matter on my own time. It's of little consequence in the grand scheme of things."

"You've promised me hell, my friend," the demon elder reminds him. "And I intend to see you deliver."

"I know what I've promised the Vig'nerash, and I know what I've promised myself. Don't worry, my friend. Neither of us will be disappointed."

There's a faint *pop* and Allensworth looks down to find thin jets of artificial fruit juice spraying the front of his surgical gown. He examines the beverage in his hand, and then the hand itself. The nails of his index and middle fingers have become long, sharp talons that are currently piercing the wax-laden surface of the juice box through both sides.

"Well, now," Allensworth passively muses, "that certainly is both unexpected and interesting."

Sircus grins a jagged-toothed grin down at him.

"Trust me, my friend, that's only the beginning."

MOONLIGHTING

Bronko is rarely the kind of boss who makes house calls, but he finds himself at the helm of a rarefied company in times even more rarefied than normal (that most relative and fluid of concepts). He hikes the cracked brick steps of Moon's Jamaica walk-up in Queens, his knees creaking like a device used by an overly enthusiastic sound effects artist in the earliest days of cinema. Having been reared in a land of ranch-style homes, he finds that ascending stairs to reach a front door never fails to elicit a barely audible stream of curses that crisscrosses several dialects. Even after living in New York City for so many years, he's never come to appreciate the aesthetic appeal or architectural necessity of the stoop.

He knocks and Moon's door is opened by Cupid, the demon ex-assassin transmogrified to personify a horrific version of love's cherubic messenger who recently went AWOL from Hell after failing his mission to kill Moon, and who subsequently became Moon's roommate.

Rarefied times, indeed.

Cupid turns his gruesomely bloated face up at Bronko.

A lit joint is hanging precariously from his perpetually puckered lips. The lazy and sporadic fluttering of the creature's miniature wings slowly disperses a cloud of sickly redolent smoke.

"Is he here?" Bronko asks blandly.

Cupid nods rapidly several times, jostling the tiny burning scroll of paper hanging from his mouth. He eagerly steps aside and opens the door, motioning for Bronko to come inside.

If Moon's apartment is ordinarily a Dumpster, it has recently become a Dumpster that also doubles as a hobo's toilet. Half the takeout food in the borough has apparently come here to die and to slowly, and excruciatingly to the senses, decompose. The entire space is one unyielding dirty-clothes hamper, and the cloying smell of bong water clings to the walls as if sprayed there by industrial jets. Bronko has seen the inside of last night's fondue pots that were more appealing as a living space.

Moon is curled into one corner of his trash-bin front room, wedged between the wall and his towering shelves of video game consoles and other high-end audiovisual electronics. His knees stop just short of his chin, which is covered in a full week's worth of stubble as opposed to his regular three to four days of neglect. His eyes are raw and red and dry after shedding every tear the moisture in his body could manufacture.

Bronko steps on and cracks the plastic case of a copy of *Red Dead Redemption 2* for PlayStation while crossing the room. He kicks it from his path, annoyed.

Behind him, Cupid flitters over the back of the couch and settles down atop a mound of plastic Chinese food containers and crumpled energy drink cans.

"I'd ask your blessing to sit down, but I don't wanna stick to any of this shit," Bronko bluntly informs Moon.

Moon doesn't look up from his stupor.

Bronko sighs. "I got a million things to worry about just now, Moon. Every blessed soul who works for Sin du Jour might be dead tomorrow, for all I know."

Moon only smooths back his greasy, unkempt hair with his fingers methodically. He continues staring at nothing.

Bronko frowns, reluctantly bending his knees and hunkering down toward the refuse-scattered floor to seek Moon's level.

"Listen here, boy. We're juiced into something way too big for a line of cooks and a couple of cut-rate magicians, and that something is closing in like a big damn vice around us all. I have to figure a way around that, and the usual way I get around things ain't gonna work this time, because I just helped stab him in the back, and I'm talkin' literally here. We're a man down and one of my kids may never come back from whatever dark place he's been cast down into. It's on me to fix all of it, and I don't have a single damn clue how to go about it.

"And despite these many urgent and dire matters, I found myself lying awake all night, trying to decide what to do with your skinny little ass."

Moon finally looks up at him.

His voice is the rasp of a ghost as he asks, "I guess I'm fired, huh?"

"I thought about that," Bronko admits. "I don't believe there's a scenario or possibility I didn't ponder. I thought about firing you. I thought about just beating you till blood came a-gushin' out your damn eyes. That one appealed to me for the better part of an hour, although in the end, I had to admit to myself I was projecting an awful lot that had nothing to do with you onto that image. I thought about giving you a stack of hundreds to blow town and alleviate my guilt and wishin' you luck as you disappeared over the bridge. Then something entirely new occurred to me, and I had to put all of my pondering on hold. Do you want to know what occurred to me, Moon?"

"I feel like you're going to tell me anyway."

"I am. It occurred to me that as much as I've yelled at you over the years, I never once asked you anything about yourself. That led me to the notion I really don't know a damn thing about you. Who are your people,

Moon? Where're you from?"

Moon shows his first emotion since Bronko entered the apartment, and that feeling is annoyance. "What difference does it make? Why does that matter right now?"

"It matters because I'm askin', and I wouldn't choose this particular moment to argue with me, were I you."

"I'm from some shitty little town in north Cali," Moon explains impatiently. "My folks were white trash morons and I haven't seen or heard from 'em in years. The end."

"Ritter said he found you down in Mexico going head-to-head against some kinda witch in a contest eatin' chupacabra guts. That true?"

"Yeah."

"You ever had a real job before you came to Sin du Jour?"

"No."

"Was that the first time you had folks placin' bets on you chokin' down some bit of awful magic?"

"No."

Bronko nods. "Tell me about it."

Moon lets his head fall back against the wall, hard enough to create a hollow thud. He closes his eyes and sighs reluctantly.

"When I was twelve, my old man was into a band of Travelers for a lot of cash. Some shanty Irish bullshit dice game. Maybe they cheated him; maybe he was just a dumbass. Neither would surprise me. Anyway, they dragged my sister and me out of bed one morning, three of them. My folks were already in the kitchen, my mom lookin' shell-shocked. There was a steaming bowl of brown stuff on the table with two spoons next to it. The Travelers called it 'debtor's stew.' It just looked like regular beef stew out of a can. I guess they put some bad Irish juju in it from the old country. They said they were gonna make me and my sister take a bite for every hundred bucks my old man owed them."

Bronko's eyes begin to darken. "What did your pa do?"

"He never even once looked at us, me or her. I remember he stared straight ahead. He wasn't just . . . not looking at us; he was trying not to see us. It was like he decided we were already dead, so it was easier on him to pretend we weren't even there, like we didn't never exist."

"What happened, Moon?"

"They started with Sunny. That was her name, my sister. The old man said it was because they made me at night and her during the day. So, we both started off life as a bad joke right off. Sunny was a few years younger than me. She didn't really know what was happening, I don't think. When they told her to eat it, she did what she was told. The first bite . . . it was like watchin' the air let out of a fucking balloon. By her third bite, she looked like . . . like Silly Putty stretched over a skeleton.

She never made it to the fourth bite. The stew, like, sucked the life right out of her."

Bronko stares at him, unhinged.

"Jesus, boy."

Moon barely hears him. He's become lost in his own story.

"My mom lost her shit, but they just slapped her around until she shut up. They had to hold me down and pinch my nose closed. It tasted like a corpse's ball sack. Nothin' happened to me, though. But the three guys who made me eat the stew . . . it bounced back on them. What happened to Sunny happened to them, right there in the kitchen, only it was . . . worse. I don't know why. But when it was over . . . when they were all . . . whatever . . . my old man finally looked at me again. He finally . . . It was like the first time in my life he actually *saw* me. But not really. It wasn't me he saw; it was . . . I might as well have been a fucking racehorse or a mean-ass dog he could fight against other dogs for cash."

"What happened?"

"He started taking me to bars, the regular human kind at first, and then he found the other kind. He'd bet anyone who'd take his action, and I'd eat whatever they put in front of me, as fast as I could. I learned quick what happened when I said no. They buried what was left of Sunny in our backyard. They didn't even say any words over the grave, didn't mark it with anything. They never told anybody. They never talked about her again. It was like she was never even fucking born."

"I'm truly sorry, son," Bronko says, and he means it.

Moon shrugs. "When I was seventeen, my mom finally swallowed a handful of pills. The old man found her barely breathing, drove her to the emergency room. I don't know if she made it or not. I stole three grand from where he stashed his cash in his toolbox and I took off. That was the last time I saw them."

"You didn't have a soul in this world to look out for you ever, did you?"

Moon stares up at Bronko. "I'm not lookin' for your sympathy."

"I ain't offerin' any. But it does explain a lot."

"Yeah? Like what?"

"Moon, I look around at this hog trough you live in and all these games you play with, and I think you're a little kid that didn't never grow up because no one taught him how. In that light, it seems wrong of me to expect you to act like a man."

"Thanks, I guess?"

"I can see you're all cut up over Hara, and rightly so. I can see I don't need to explain your part in it or how you let your team down because you already know. I can further see I can't punish you any harder than you're punishin' yourself. I could try, but it'd just be to make me feel better."

"What do you want from me, man?"

Bronko fixes him with a hard stare, the same one that's had many a line cook pissing down their leg.

Moon corrects himself. "What do you want from me, *Chef*?"

Bronko grunts, satisfied. "I ain't gonna fire you, Moon. What I'm going to do is bench your ass. You're off Ritter's team until you earn your place on it."

"How do I do that?"

"By doing two things I expect you've never done in your life. The first is following through on something you start. The second is doin' as you're fuckin' well told. I gave you a job to do. You're gonna do that job. You're gonna climb up Ryland's ass until that alky teaches you every damn thing he knows."

"What if I can't?"

"*Then* I'll fire you."

Bronko stands, turning to leave the apartment. He pauses as he confronts Moon's costly shrine to video gaming. The executive chef calmly reaches up and pulls down the monolithic television obscuring most of the wall. Its top crashes against the overburdened coffee table, collapsing its legs and sending fast food wrappers and head shop paraphernalia flying in all directions. The screen of the television itself is shattered, and its wires yank down half a dozen assorted pieces of equipment as well.

Cupid flitters several feet above the couch, shaking a fist angrily at Bronko, who ignores him.

Moon doesn't even stir. He only watches his employer passively.

"Get rid of all this shit," Bronko says, waving a hand in front of the gaming consoles. "Time to grow up, boy. And clean this shit pen. Start there. That's an order."

Moon blinks up at Bronko, the expression on his face as open and vulnerable as anyone at Sin du Jour has ever seen.

"Chef? D'you ... do you think they'd want to ... y'know, work with me again, or whatever? Ritter and Cindy?"

Bronko doesn't answer at first. Instead, he plucks the joint from Cupid's mouth and takes a hit, drawing in the acrid smoke and releasing it with relish like an old pro, or perhaps an aging roadie.

"Cataracts," he explains in a momentarily constricted voice, handing the joint back to the demon.

To Moon he says, "I think all they want is to see you give a shit. And sayin' it ain't never gonna be enough. You have to show them."

Bronko leaves him with that, exiting the filthy apartment and slamming the front door shut behind him.

Cupid, still hovering amidst the spastic beating of his undersized wings, watches the executive chef go. After he's gone, the demon turns toward Moon, puffing on the half-burnt joint.

"What?" Moon asks.

Cupid frantically waves his stubby arms above the broken flatscreen.

Moon sighs. "Like he said, dude. It's time to grow up."

SINS OF THE MORNING

The new day is a lover's lane cop shining their aluminum flashlight through a misted car window. There's the feeling of surprise and confusion and the acid, convex edge of shame as that damning light irradiates Ritter's closed eyelids. They trip over the contrary acts of opening and blinking simultaneously, remaining locked in a vibrating stalemate that stabs his temples. Ritter has to grind his knuckles against his eyelids for several seconds before they'll allow themselves to be peeled back. He turns away from his open bedroom window, propping himself up on one elbow and blinking the world into focus.

Lena sits on the end of the bed, arms encircling her scabbed knees. Like him, she's naked, and there are bruises on her back and shoulders and neck, purple slowly fading to yellow and green, souvenirs from the wreckage of Gluttony Bay. She also has a tattoo above her right hip Ritter hasn't noticed before. He's traced with lips and fingertips the army ink on her right bicep, *Mountain* in scroll above two crossed swords. She also has her military discharge date on her left side and a black shadow kitchen knife along her right calf. He's spent time examining all three, but this fourth design eluded him somehow.

Ritter cocks his head, eyeing the colored ink rising just above the crest of her hip near her back. *Fight like a girl* is written in a circle of black, white, and red script.

"How bad is it?" Ritter asks her.

Lena isn't the least bit startled by his voice. She neither turns her body nor looks back at him, continuing to stare at the blank wall.

"How bad is what?"

He shrugs. "Everything, I guess."

"I'm sore and I had bad dreams, and I'm scared for Darren, and worried about what's going to happen now, to all of us."

"I don't know what's going to happen, but I'll help Darren if you'll let me."

"You'll help Darren because you owe it to *him*, not me."

"You're right."

She peers over her shoulder at him then, eyes tragic and beautiful and framed by the sleep tangles of her short dark hair.

"I can't forgive you," she tells him. "Not for what you did to Darren, and not for what you did before."

"I'd never ask you for forgiveness."

"I can't forget, either. If you were counting on that, it's not going to happen."

"I would never expect you to forget anything."

"Rationally . . . like, on a purely intellectual level, I know you're not an evil man. I don't even think you're a bad man. I see your remorse and your guilt. I know it's real. I know you take care of all those witches in Williamsburg without them even knowing it. I know why you do it. I see the way you care about the people around you and how you'd do anything for them. I believe you care about me. I know all that stuff, but it doesn't . . . There's still this part of me that isn't rational or logical and that part just wants to hate the fuck out of you, you know? It hates the things you've done and wants you to suffer for those things."

"I could tell you I do, every day, but it's not nearly as much as I deserve."

"I'd believe you, but it wouldn't change anything."

"Are you sorry you're here?"

"Yes, and also no."

Lena looks away, rubbing her face with both of her palms until she can summon the words to express the boil of thoughts threatening to overflow her mind.

"When I came back from Kabul, I didn't want to keep in touch with anyone from my division, not even on fucking Facebook. It's not that they were all assholes; it's just . . . I didn't need to rehash everything that happened over there and I didn't want to be made to think about it all the time. But then, sometimes, you need to be with somebody who understands, and nobody back here really understands, least of all Darren. You can't explain to someone who wasn't there what it was like, or why you are the way you are because of it. You can try, and they'll nod and their eyes will be all full of sympathy and they'll repeat some shit they heard or read somewhere, but they can never get it. I like that you get it, and that you don't remind me of being back there."

"I do know a bit about seeing a bunch of shit no one should have to see, even if it wasn't the same shit you saw."

Lena sighs. "I don't know what I'm trying to get at here. I'm not making excuses for threatening you with a knife one day and then fucking you the next. And I'm grateful you came to save us and take us out of that place, but that's not why this happened either. It's just . . . Everything is too ugly and too temporary to live every day pissed off at the people you like, even if you have cause."

Ritter doesn't say anything. He has questions but no intention of asking them.

She looks back at him again. "You never said you were sorry for any of it."

"Do you want me to?"

Lena shakes her head. "No."

"It doesn't fix anything," he says.

"I know that. I'm glad you do, too."

"The only real penance I know of is living with it."

Lena rolls to her left, turning and crawling up the bed alongside his body. She lies down and rests her cheek on his stomach, closing her eyes.

"I don't want to talk anymore," she whispers.

Ritter nods, silent. He deftly and gently begins smoothing the tangles from her hair with his fingertips.

The sun seems less harsh now, and the two of them stay like that until the light across the bed turns to shadow.

EPILOGUE: DESERT RIDER

"The truth is, I don't know a single detail about Hara's life," Ritter confesses.

He's standing before the entirety of Sin du Jour's staff. They've all convened on the roof of the building to say good-bye to the fallen member of their intrepid Stocking & Receiving Department. His body has been cleaned, wrapped in hemp shrouds, and dressed in a gargantuan mahogany casket built by Ritter and Marcus's own hands.

The only ones absent are Darren and James—Darren who is still recovering from his ordeal, and James who refuses to leave him—and Moon. No one specifically excluded Moon from the proceedings; they didn't have to, as Moon was more than happy in his shame to exclude himself.

"I saved it once. Hara's life. A long time ago. He felt he owed me for that. He would've followed me to the fire at the end of the world if I asked him to. That's who he was, and that's what he believed. But I can't tell you where he came from, or who his people were, what he did or where he'd been that brought him to the point in his life when we met. I don't know about any of that. I don't imagine there's a living soul on this planet who does."

Standing closest to the coffin, Cindy's eyes are dry. Anger is her version of grief, and the scowl she wears is for Allensworth, for Moon, but more than anything for death itself.

"But I do know who Hara was," Ritter continues. "And I think that's more important. He had the sharpest mind I've ever encountered, but he never spoke unless he had something to say. He was a desert rider. He always returned to the desert. That existence appealed to him because there are no false pretenses among desert riders. They live simple. They live honestly. They live in motion, in a confluence of circles that always bring them back to the beginning. Hara found purity in that. I wish we could all be so content."

Not everyone chooses rage. Lena weeps for the stoic giant, and for a lot of other things. Nikki cries the same tears she'd pour for any of them, all of them.

Even Bronko feels the hot, wet sting on his cheeks.

"I'm not sad for my friend. I'm sad for myself, and for the rest of us left behind. We're left without him, and still in danger, still with wars to fight. Hara is beyond that now. He's found the peace that eludes the rest of us. And I'm happy for him because of that."

Ritter finishes speaking. He turns and walks behind the casket, reaching inside his pocket and removing the key to Hara's Gunbus motorcycle. He kisses the brass and places it atop the lid.

As they all stand in silence for the departed, Ritter joins Lena and Cindy, bowing his head with the rest.

Instead of thinking about Hara, Ritter imagines somewhere in the world at that moment, there's a rare and much-needed rain falling on distant sand.

He hopes something grows there, the way it can't grow in the city.

Acknowledgments

This is the penultimate volume in the Sin du Jour series, yet I haven't run out of folks to thank; indeed, the list grows longer with each book. My thanks to my editor, Lee Harris, for the explodey things and for cleaning up my big messes. My copy editor, Richard Shealy, for cleaning up a lot more of my little messes. My agent, DongWon, who keeps me on point. My fiancée, Nikki, who keeps me on point when nothing else, including my agent, can possibly do the job. Irene Gallo and Peter Lutjen, who just keep topping themselves with each cover they produce for Sin du Jour. Tor.com Pub's swag master, Mordicai Knode, and ace marketing whiz, Katharine Duckett, who keep pushing to bring the books in this series to the attention of the masses. I also want to thank Sue and Del Howison of Dark Delicacies in Burbank, who continually invite me to celebrate the releases of these books in their amazing shop. My mother, who drives all the way from Phoenix and rallies everyone she's ever met to fill my book signings, just in case. Finally and most important, thank you, Sin du Jour's regular customers, whose visits keep the lights on the stoves burning. I'll see you for the final course.

About the Author

Photograph by Earl Newton

MATT WALLACE is the author of the Sin du Jour Affairs, *The Next Fix*, *The Failed Cities*, and the novella series Slingers. He's also penned more than one hundred short stories, some of which have won awards and been nominated for others, in addition to writing for film and television. In his youth, he traveled the world as a professional wrestler and unarmed combat and self-defense instructor before retiring to write full-time. He now resides in Los Angeles with the love of his life and inspiration for Sin du Jour's resident pastry chef.

TOR·COM

Science fiction. Fantasy. The universe.

And related subjects.

*

More than just a publisher's website, *Tor.com*
is a venue for **original fiction, comics,** and
discussion of the entire field of SF and fantasy,
in all media and from all sources. Visit our site
today—and join the conversation yourself.